CONTEMPORARY AMERICAN FICTION

SPIRITS

Richard Bausch was born in Fort Benning, Georgia. He is the author of three novels—*Real Presence, Take Me Back*, and *The Last Good Time*—and has published short stories in *The Atlantic Monthly* and other magazines. He lives in Fairfax, Virginia, with his wife, Karen, and their four children.

RICHARD BAUSCH

SPIRITS

AND OTHER STORIES

PENGUIN BOOKS

PENGUIN BOOKS
Published by the Penguin Group
Viking Penguin Inc., 40 West 23rd Street,
New York, New York 10010, U.S.A.
Penguin Books Ltd, 27 Wrights Lane,
London W8 5TZ, England
Penguin Books Australia Ltd, Ringwood,
Victoria, Australia
Penguin Books Canada Ltd, 2801 John Street,
Markham, Ontario, Canada L3R 1B4
Penguin Books (N.Z.) Ltd, 182–190 Wairau Road,
Auckland 10, New Zealand

Penguin Books Ltd, Registered Offices:
Harmondsworth, Middlesex, England

First published in the United States of America by
The Linden Press/Simon and Schuster 1987
Published in Penguin Books 1988

These short stories are works of fiction. Names, characters, places, and
incidents either are the product of the author's imagination or are used
fictitiously. Any resemblance to actual events or locales or persons, living or
dead, is entirely coincidental.

"All the Way in Flagstaff, Arizona," "What Feels Like the World," "Police
Dreams," and "The Man Who Knew Belle Starr" appeared in *The Atlantic
Monthly*; "The Wife's Tale" appeared, in slightly different form, in
Ploughshares; "Contrition" appeared in *The New Virginia Review*.

LIBRARY OF CONGRESS CATALOGING IN PUBLICATION DATA
Bausch, Richard, 1945–
Spirits, and other stories.
I. Title.
[PS3552.A846S6 1988]   813'.54   88-5853
ISBN 0 14 01.0963 3

Printed in the United States of America by
R. R. Donnelley & Sons Company, Harrisonburg, Virginia
Set in Plantin

I AM GRATEFUL TO THE JOHN SIMON GUGGEN-
HEIM MEMORIAL FOUNDATION FOR A FELLOWSHIP
IN FICTION, WHICH HAS PROVIDED ME WITH
NEEDED TIME AND SUPPORT DURING THE WRITING
OF THIS BOOK.

*In memory of Barbara Bausch Moody (1943–1974)
and Helen Simmons Bausch (1919–1985),
for their children, and for Karen with love.*

CONTENTS

"Ja, Geist ist alles."
—FREUD

"Likewise the Spirit also helpeth our infirmities: for we know not what we should pray for as we ought: but the Spirit itself maketh intercession for us with sighs too deep for words."
—ST. PAUL TO THE ROMANS, 8:26

SPIRITS
AND OTHER STORIES

ALL THE WAY IN FLAGSTAFF, ARIZONA

Sitting in the shaded cool quiet of St. Paul's Church in Flagstaff, Walter remembers a family picnic. This memory is two years old, but nothing ever fades from it. It takes place in a small park called Hathaway Forest, on Long Island, one Sunday afternoon in early summer. He and his wife, Irene, spread blankets on the grass next to a picnic table and a brick barbecue pit; it is a warm, clear-blue day, with a breeze. Irene has insisted that they all go, as a family, and so soccer games, trips to the movies and to the houses of friends, have been put aside. Because Walter is hung over, he tries to beg off, but she will not hear of it; she will not cater to his hangovers anymore, she tells him. So they all go. He and Irene sit quietly on the blankets as, in the grass field before them, the children run—William, the oldest, hanging back a little, making a sacrifice of pretending to have a good time: he is planning for the priesthood these days, wants to be Gregory Peck in *The Keys of the Kingdom*. He saw the movie on television a year ago and now his room is full of books on China, on the lives of the saints, the missionaries, the martyrs. Every morning he goes to Mass and Communion. Walter feels embarrassed in his company, especially when William shows this saintly, willing face to the world.

"I wonder if it would help William to discover masturbation," Walter says. "He's at that age, isn't he? Don't boys start at fourteen? When did I start? I guess I should remember."

"I forgot the baked beans," Irene says. "I left them sitting in the middle of the kitchen counter." She has this way of not hearing him when she wants to avoid a subject; she will not talk about William. "You want some lemonade?"

"No, thanks." He makes a face; she smiles. He can always make her laugh.

The children form a ring, and begin to move in a circle. Susan, the second child, orchestrates this, calling in a kind of singing cadence as they contract and expand the ring by raising and lowering their arms. They are playing well together, cooperating; even William seems to have forgotten about heaven and hell for the moment, moving a little too fast for the youngest, the baby, Carol, to keep up with him. There is something mischievous about the way he causes the girl to falter and lose her hold on him.

"You should light the charcoal, honey," Irene says.

"Certainly," he says. He is anxious to please. He knows she will again have to ask her father for money, and she will again use the word *borrow*. There is always the hope that something will change. He stands over the brick barbecue pit and pours charcoal, while she pours more lemonade, not bothering to ask him this time if he wants any. In the car, in the space under the spare tire, hidden by a half-used roll of paper towels, is a fifth of Jim Beam. He thinks of it with something bordering on erotic anticipation, though his head feels as if it were webbed with burning wires. As he sprinkles lighter fluid on the coals, he begins to plan how he will get to the bottle without the others knowing he has done so.

"Dad."

It is William, standing a little apart from Susan and the younger children. He holds up a Nerf football, wanting to pass it.

Walter smiles. "I'm cooking. I'm the chef of the day."

William wants to get a game up, boys against the girls; he wants Irene to play. She refuses, cheerfully, and so does Susan, and the younger boys begin a desultory game of keep away from Carol, who begins to take it seriously, crying and demanding that she be given a chance to throw and catch the ball. William and Susan walk off toward the far edge of the woods, talking, William pausing now and then to pick up and throw a stone or a piece of wood. Irene sits reading a magazine, with a pad and pencil on her lap. She likes to write down the recipes she finds, and keeps the pad for this purpose. In fact, she doesn't read these magazines as much as she ransacks them, looking for things to save. She's a frugal woman; she's had to be. She controls the money now, what there is of it. Since the last hitch in the Army, Walter has worked seven different jobs; now, at forty-six, he's night clerk in a 7-Eleven store.

"That's enough," Irene calls to the two younger boys, Brad and James, who have tormented Carol to the point of a tantrum. Carol is lying on her stomach, beating her fists into the grass, while they toss the ball above her head, keeping it just out of reach. "Brad! Bra-a-a-a-d! James!"

The two boys stop, finally, walk away scuffing the ground. In a moment they are running across the field, and Carol has come crying to her mother. Because she is the youngest and the smallest, she has learned to be feisty and short-tempered; she seems somehow always dogged, face into the wind, dauntless. "Don't pay any attention to them," Irene is saying.

Walter lights the fire, stands watching it.

"You go on, now, and play," Irene says, and Carol whines that she doesn't want to, she wants to stay here. "No—now, go on. Go have fun. I don't want you hanging back all afternoon. Go on—go."

Carol wanders over to a little play area near the car; it is, in fact, too near: it will be hard for Walter to get anything out of the trunk if she stays where she is, riding a sea dragon on a corkscrew-like metal spring.

"I don't like her being over there by herself," Walter says.

"She's fine," says Irene. "Let her alone."

He sits down, rubs his hands; he wants a drink.

"You want to put the hot dogs on sticks?" Irene asks.

"That tire's low," he says.

"No, it's not."

"It is—look. Look at it. It's low. I better change it."

"You're in no shape to change a tire."

He gets up. "I think it's low."

"Walter."

"I'm just going to look at it."

"Hi, Daddy," Carol says as he approaches.

"Go see your mother."

"I'm riding the dragon."

"Your mother wants you."

"I don't wanna."

"Come on," he says, "I have to look at this tire." He lifts her from the dragon, puts her down on her feet, or tries to: she raises her legs, so that he comes close to falling forward; he lifts again, tries again to set her down, and it's as if they dance. "Stop it," he says, "stand up." She laughs, and he sets her suddenly, with a bump, down on her rear end. "Now you can sit there," he says. She begins to cry. He walks over to the car and stands gazing at the right rear tire, which is not low enough. Even so, he opens the trunk, glances back at Irene, who is lying on the blanket like a sunbather now, her arms straight at her sides, her eyes closed. Carol still whines and cries, sitting in the dust in the foreground.

"Go on," Walter says, "you're not hurt."

"Carol," Irene calls without moving, "come here."

Walter is already reaching into the little well beneath the spare. The Beam is wrapped in a paper bag, and carefully he removes it, leaning into the hot space. In almost the same motion, he has broken the seal on the bottle and held the lip of it to his mouth, swallowing. He caps it, peers out at Irene and

Carol, who are frozen for him in a sort of tableau: Carol beginning to move toward her mother, and Irene lying face up to the sun. He leans in, takes another swallow, caps the bottle again and sets it down, rattles the jack, stands back slowly and puts his hands on his hips.

"Walter."

"It's okay," he calls. "I guess it'll have to do—the spare's no better." He looks at Irene, sees that Carol has reached her, that she is involved with Carol, who wants her to fix and bow her hair. So he leans into the trunk again, swallows more of the whiskey. Then he recaps the bottle one more time, puts it back in its place, retrieves it almost immediately, and takes still another swallow. He closes the trunk hard, walks steadily across to the blanket, where Irene and Carol are busy trying to get Carol's hair braided and bowed. He sits down, looks at the flames licking low along the whitening coals. When Carol asks him to look at how pretty her hair is, he tells her she is the most beautiful little girl he ever saw. He reaches for her, pulls her to him, and hugs her. "You are my sweet sweet sweet sweet thing," he says, "You are my sweetie-pie. My little baby love darling boost-a-booter."

"I love you, Daddy."

She removes herself from him, dances, for his benefit, in a circle around the blanket. Then she runs off to meet William and Susan, who are coming across the crest of the field.

"IT could be like this all the time," Irene says.

He says "Yeah." He gets up, stands over the fire. "The coals are almost ready."

"What's the mat—" she begins.

He has swayed only slightly; he pretends to have simply lost his balance on an unevenness in the ground, looks at his feet, lifts one leg, puts it down. It is a beautiful blurred world, and he believes he can do anything.

"It's brave of you to come out today," she says.

"I wanted to."

"You know, Walter, I am going to leave you."

"Right now?"

She ignores this. "I don't want to. I love you. But I really am. You don't believe me, Walter, because you've never believed me. But this time you're wrong. In a while, very soon, I'm going to take the children and go."

"But don't you see?" he says. "I'm going to quit. I'm never touching the stuff again."

"No," she says.

"Come on, kid," he says.

"Let me tell you, dear, what you were thinking all the way here, and what you finally got your hands on a few minutes ago. You were thinking all the time, weren't you, about the bottle of booze you had stashed in the trunk of the car."

"What bottle of booze?"

"I believe it was Jim Beam?" She looks at him.

He wonders if she can see the color changing in his face and neck, the blood rushing there. "Jim Beam," he says. "Jim Beam."

"It won't work, Walter."

"You think that's it? You think I've been—you think that's what I've been doing, huh." He is nodding, looking away from her, trying to control his voice. "You think—on a beautiful day like this, when I'm with my family—some—a bottle of booze in the trunk—"

"Forget it," she says.

"I didn't know—I didn't even know if there was a bottle of booze in the goddamn spare-tire well."

"Please," she says.

"You think I've been thinking about a goddamn bottle of booze in the trunk of the car."

"All right, then."

"That's what you think of me. I mean—we've come that far

—that you'd think I could be standing here on this nice day thinking about sneaking drinks like there's some—like there's a problem or something—"

"Walter," she says.

"I mean like it wasn't just—you know, a drink in the afternoon or something—"

"Don't say any more," she tells him.

"Just something I found and—you think I haven't been sick at heart for what I've done, Irene." He has never meant anything more. "I didn't even think anything about it, honey—you think I'd do anything to hurt you or the kids—something—some bottle or something that's supposed to be hidden or something. Like I planned it or something. I swear I just remembered it was there—I didn't—didn't want to worry you, Irene —Irene—"

"The sad thing," Irene says, "is that I could've stopped you today—just now. I knew what you were doing—after all, Walter, you've become a bit sloppy in your various deceptions and ruses. They've become pretty transparent. I could've stopped you, only I just—I just didn't have the energy."

"I don't know what you're talking about," he says. He looks at his children, all of them coming now from the crest; they seem somehow not together, though they come in a group, no more than five feet apart.

"I wish I could feel anything but this exhaustion," Irene says.

"It's not anything like I'm drunk or anything," Walter says. "I just need to get calmed down, honey."

"No," she says.

"You know me, Irene. I always—haven't I always come through?"

She looks at him. "I think—now—that you think you have."

"I just need a little time," he says.

"Walter."

"That's all, honey. Just let me get straight a little." He doesn't want to talk anymore. He drops down at her side. "I'm nervous, kid. I get real bad nervous—and—and I'm not going to drink anymore. I'm simply—absolutely done with it. Forever, Renie. Okay? I'm going to pull it together this time." As he gazes out at the field, at his children returning, he is full of resolve, and courage. Irene sighs, pats his shoulder, and then takes his hand into her own. "Poor Walter," she says, "so sick."

"I'll be all right," he says. "I just need to be calm."

The children are there now, and the picnic is made ready: William puts hot dogs on the grill, and Susan dishes out potato salad, Jell-O, bread, pickles. There is a lot of vying for attention, a lot of energy and noise. It all rises around Walter and his wife, who do not look at each other.

ANYONE walking into St. Paul's at this hour will see a man sitting in the last pew, hands folded neatly in his lap. He sits very straight, with dignity, though his clothes are soiled and disheveled. In his mind are the voices of two years ago, the quality of light on that day, and how the breezes blew, fragrant and warm. He can hear the voices.

"Oh," William says, shortly before they start to eat. "We forgot to say grace."

"It's too late now," Susan says.

"It's not too late. It can't ever be too late."

"It's too late."

"It's not too late—that's just silly, Susan."

"Daddy, isn't it too late?"

"It's not too late," Irene says. "William, go ahead."

"Bless us, O Lord, and these Thy gifts which we are about to receive from Thy bounty, through Christ our Lord, amen."

"I still say it was too late," Susan says.

Irene says, "Susan."

"I've decided I'm going to be a nun," Susan says.

"Susan—that's nothing to joke about."

"It's not a joke. I'm going to be a nun and wear icky black

clothes and have my hair cut off at the roots and sit in church
with my hands open in my lap and sing off tune like Sister
Marie does."

"That's a sacrilege," William says.

"What's a sacrilege?" Brad asks.

"It's when you talk like Susan," says William.

"A sacrilege," says Susan, "is when you take Holy Communion with a mortal sin on your soul."

"And when you say you're going to be a nun when you're
not," William says.

"Come on now, kids," Walter says, "let's get off each other
a little. Let's talk about something nice."

"I know," says Brad, "let's talk about Pac-Man."

"Who wants to talk about *that*," says Carol.

"All I said was I was going to be a nun," Susan says, "and
everybody gets crazy. Mostly Saint William. You should've
heard Saint William a little while ago, planning his martyrdom
in China—shot by the Commies. Right, William?"

"That's enough," Walter says. "Let him alone. Let's everybody let everybody else alone. Jesus."

"Have mercy on us," William mutters.

"Oh, look," Walter says, "don't do that. Don't pray when I
talk."

Irene says, "Let's just eat quietly, all right?"

"Well, he keeps praying around me. Jesus, I *hate* that."

"Have mercy on us," says William.

"When're you leaving for China, son?"

"You don't have to make fun of me."

"Okay, look—let's all start over. Jesus." Walter spins around,
to catch William moving his lips. "Jesus Jesus Jesus Jesus
Jesus," he says.

William crosses himself.

"Amazing. The kid's amazing."

"Let's all please just stop it and eat. Can we please just do
that?"

Susan says, "I've changed my mind about being a nun. I'm going to be a priest."

"Oh," William says, "that *is* a sacrilege."

"William," says Walter, "will you please pronounce the excommunications so we can all go to hell in peace?"

"I don't even like this family," the boy mutters.

"Perhaps you should've asked your Father in heaven to have chosen another family for you to be raised in on your trek to the cross."

"Have mercy."

"I don't believe I used any profanity that last time."

"Have mercy on us," William mutters.

"All right!" Irene shouts. "We're going to eat and stop all this arguing and bickering. Please, Walter."

"You might address your displeasure to the Christ, here. Or is it the Vicar of Christ?"

"Have mercy on us."

"I'll be the first lady priest in the Catholic Church," Susan says, "and then I'll get married."

Walter says "Don't pay any attention to her, William. Think of her as a cross to bear."

"Walter," Irene says.

He stands. "Okay. Truce. No more teasing and no more bickering. We are a family, right? We have to stick together and tolerate each other sometimes."

They are looking at him. He touches his own face, where his mouth, his lips are numb. His eyes feel swollen.

"And then," Susan says, "after I'm married, I'll become Pope."

Walter bursts into laughter as William turns to Susan and says, "You are committing a mortal sin."

"Susan!" Irene says.

Walter says, "Judge not, lest ye be judged, William, my boy."

"I know what a mortal sin is," Brad says.

"Everybody knows that," says James.

"Look for the mote, William. When you see the gleam, look for the mote," Walter is saying.

William mutters, "I don't even know what that means."

"Walter, sit down," Irene says. "Let him alone. All of you let him alone."

"Let's all leave each other alone, that's right," Walter says. He sits down. They eat quietly for a while, and he watches them. Irene wipes mustard from Carol's mouth, from the front of her dress. William's eyes are glazed, and he eats furiously, not looking at anyone. He has been caught out in his pride, Walter thinks, has been shown to himself as less perfect than the glorious dream of a movie he wants to live. It dawns on Walter that his son probably prays for him, since he does not go to church. He wonders, now, what they all think of that, of the fact that he is, by every tenet of their religion, bound for hell. This makes him laugh.

"What?" Irene says. "Tell me."

"Nothing. I was—" He thinks for a moment. "I was thinking about this one," pointing to Susan, "planning to be a married lady priest."

Susan beams under his gaze.

And then he looks at William, feels sorry. "It's okay, William," he says, "it's all in fun."

The boy continues to eat.

"William."

Irene touches Walter's wrist.

"No," Walter says, "the kid can accept somebody's—a gesture—can't he? My God."

William crosses himself again.

Walter stands. "That's the last time."

"Father Boyer, at church," William says almost defiantly, "he told us to do it whenever someone used the Lord's name—"

Walter interrupts him. "I don't care what Father Boyer said. I'm bigger than Father Boyer. I can beat the *shit* out of Father Boyer."

"Not another word from anyone!" Irene shouts.

For a moment no one says anything.

"Well," Walter says, "aren't we a happy bunch?"

James says, "What do you expect?"

"Why don't you explain that one, James?"

The boy shrugs. He is always saying these mysteriously adult things that seem to refer slyly to other things, and then shrugging them off as if he is too tired to bother explaining them. Last year, at the age of eight, he announced to Irene that he did not believe in God. It was a crisis; Irene feared that something serious was wrong. James has since revised himself: he will grant the existence. Those are the words he used. Walter looks upon him with more than a little trepidation, because James is the one who most resembles him. More even than William, who, now, with his heart in the lap of God, is hard to place. Even Irene, for all her devoutness, finds William irritating at times.

"I am going to be a priest," Susan says now. "All I have to do is get them to change the rules."

"You," says Walter, "are the saint of persistence. You know what a wolverine is?"

"Some kind of wolf?"

"The wolverine kills its prey by sheer persistence. I mean, if it decided it wanted you for dinner, you could take a plane to Seattle, the wolverine would meet you at the airport, bib on, knife and fork ready, licking his chops. Salt and pepper by the plate, oregano, parsley, a beer . . ."

Susan laughs.

"Daddy's funny," Carol says.

"When I'm the first lady priest and married Pope, I'll buy a wolverine and keep it as a pet," Susan says.

"Have mercy on us," says William.

"All right," Walter says, "let's drop it, please, William. No more prayers, please. We're all right. God will forgive us, I'm sure, if we all just shut the fuck up for a while."

"Walter!"

"I'm sorry, I'm sorry," he says.

They are quiet, then, for a long time. The youngest ones, Brad and James and Carol, look at him with something like amazement. He makes two more trips to the trunk of the car, not even hiding it now, and in the end he gets Carol and James to laugh at him by making faces, miming someone sliding off a bench, pretending to be terrified of his food. Susan and William laugh too, now, as he does a man unable to get a hot dog into his mouth.

"You clown," Irene says, but she smiles.

They all laugh and talk now; the afternoon wanes that way: Walter tosses the football with William, and Brad and James chase a Frisbee with Susan and Carol. Irene sits on the picnic table, sipping her lemonade. It grows cooler, and others come to the field, and finally it's time to leave. They all work together, gathering the debris of the afternoon, and Walter packs the trunk. He's bold enough to take the bottle of Beam out of its place and drink from it—small sips, he tells Irene, offering her some. She refuses as she has always refused, but she does so with, he is sure, a smile. It strikes him that there is nothing to worry about, not a thing in the world, and he clowns with his children, makes them laugh, all the way home, Irene driving. He calls to people out the window of the car, funny things, and they are all almost hysterical with laughter. They arrive; there is the slow unwinding, getting out of the car and stretching legs and arms, and Walter begins to wrestle with Carol, bending over her, tickling her upper legs, swinging her through his own as she wriggles and laughs. Brad jumps on his back, then, and he pretends to be pulled down, rolls in the grass with the boy, and then chases him, bent over, arms dangling, like an ape's. He is hearing the delightful keening sound of his children's laughter in the shadows. It is getting dark. He chases Brad and James around to the backyard, and they are hiding there, just beyond the square lighter shape of Irene's garden. He crouches in the shadow of the house and makes an ape sound, *whooo-hooo, whooo-hooo hah-hah-hah-hah.* He can hear them talking low and he thinks, Why this is easy, this is fun. Carefully he works his way closer, seeing William and Susan running along the back fence, their silhouettes in the dusky light. *Whoo-hoo, whoo-hoo.* And now he makes his run at them, changes direction, follows Brad, while the others scatter. When he catches Brad, he carries him under his arm, kicking and struggling, to the house, the screened-in back porch, where the others have gathered and are huddling, laughing in the dark. He comes stumbling up onto the porch and he has them, they are trapped with him. He puts Brad down in the mass of struggling arms and legs; he engulfs them, kneeling; he has them all in the wide embrace of his arms; he's tickling a leg here, pinching or squeezing an arm there, roaring, gorilla-like. He catches one of them trying to get away, then turns and grabs another. He's got them all again, and they are yelling and laughing, there is light on them now, a swath of yellow light, and he looks up to see Irene's shape in the doorway, everything speeding up again, until there is a long shout, a scream.

And he stops. He stands, sees that they are cringing against the base of the porch wall, to the left of the door, cringing there and shaking, their eyes enormous, filled with tears.

"Kids?" he says.

They are sobbing, and he steps back, nearly tumbles backward out the screen door and down the stairs. "Kids?" he says.

Nobody moves.

"H-hey. Kids?"

Irene steps down, bends to help William rise. They all get up slowly, looking at him with the tremendous wariness of animals at bay.

"H-hey—it's me," he says, holding out one hand. "Kids?"

"Come on," Irene is saying, "don't be silly. Your daddy would never hurt you." She makes each of them kiss him, then ushers them inside. "Susan, will you start the bathwater?" The door closes on them. Walter looks at his hands and says "God. Oh my God." He doesn't really hear himself. And in a moment Irene opens the door and steps out lightly, closing it behind her. All around, now, the insects are starting up. Irene's voice begins softly: "We've been through so much, Walter, so much together —and I simply can't do it anymore. I don't know what to say or do anymore. I love you, but I can't make it be enough anymore." She kisses him on the side of the face, turns, and is gone.

YET it takes more than a year for her finally to leave him. She gives him every chance. She waits for him to put it together as he keeps saying he will. He tries for a while, in fact: he goes to a doctor, a psychologist specializing in family counseling, who tells him he has not broken with his father, and instructs him to find some ritual way of making the break. So he goes back to Alabama to stand over his father's grave. At first, nothing happens. He feels anger, but it is only what he expected to feel. And then there is a kind of sorrow, almost sweet, welling up in him. It makes him wince, actually take a step back from the grave as if something had moved there. When he was seven years old his father took him outside of the house in Montgomery and made him urinate on his mother's roses. He tells himself, standing over the grave in Montgomery, that children have been through worse; indeed, he himself has. Yet it takes all the moisture from his mouth, remembering it. Perhaps it is the fact that it was done to him not for himself but to get at his mother —there is something so terrifying about being used that way, merely as an instrument of wounding. In any case, it has haunted him, and now at the gravesite he spits, he rages, he tears the grass. It all seems simply ordained. It is a role he plays, watching himself play it. It exorcises nothing.

He returns from Alabama with a sense of doom riding him like a spirit, a weight on his neck, the back of his shoulders. He visits the psychologist, who seems slightly alarmed at the effect of the journey on him. He is determined, vibrant with will, and hopelessly afraid. The psychologist wants to know what his exact thought was the first time he ever picked up a drink. Walter can't remember that. His father never drank. He believes he wanted at first to show his freedom, like other boys. He says finally he wanted it to relax and be kind, to relieve some of the tensions that build in him. And so the psychologist begins to try to explore, with him, those tensions. They are many, but they all have the same root, and there is no use talking about childhood trauma and dreams: Walter is versed in the canon; his hopes are for something else. He can tell the psychologist the whole thing in a single sentence: he has always been paralyzed by the fear that he will repeat, with his own children, the pattern of his father's brutality. What he wants is for the psychologist to guarantee him that this won't happen, tell him categorically that there will be no such repetition, and of course this can't be done. Life must be lived in the uncertainty of freedom of choice, the psychologist says. The problem is that Walter is afraid to take responsibility for himself. It is all talk, and it is all true. Walter's father had a thing he liked to call "night dances," in which, for the benefit of Walter, for his correction and edification, Walter's father became a sort of dark gibbet that Walter danced beneath, held by the wrist within the small circumference, the range, of a singing swung belt whose large buckle was embossed with the head of a longhorn steer. This all took place in the basement of the house in Montgomery, before Walter was ten years old. There was no light at all in the basement, and so it was necessary for the boy to dodge blindly, and to keep from crying too loudly, so he could hear the *whoosh-whoosh* of the belt. Walter trembles to think of that. He tells the psychologist how his father would swing the belt calmly, without passion, like a machine, quiet in the dark. He shakes, telling it. He talks about the ancient story: the man who, in the act of trying to avoid some evil in himself, embraces it, creates it.

The visits end. He is dry for about two weeks, but falters, and Irene finally does leave him.

This is what has happened to him. He is in Flagstaff, Arizona. He sits gazing at the small stained-glass windows on either side of the church, where in a few minutes he will probably be talking to a priest. God, he thinks, Flagstaff, Arizona. There is no reason for it. Perhaps he will go somewhere else, too. There is no telling where he might wind up. Irene and the children are all the way in Atlanta, Georgia, with Irene's parents. He has not had anything to drink today, and his hands shake, so he looks at them. He wonders if he should wait to talk to a priest, if he should tell a priest anything, or just ask for some food, maybe. He wonders if maybe he shouldn't tell the priest about the day of the picnic that he has been remembering so vividly, when Irene came out on the porch and told him she couldn't make it be enough anymore. He wonders if he should talk about it: how he walked out to the very edge of the lawn and turned to look upon the lighted windows of the house, thinking of the people inside, whom he had named and loved and called sons, daughters, wife. How he had stood there trembling, shaking as from a terrific chill, while the dark, the night, came.

WISE MEN
AT THEIR END

THEODORE WEATHERS WOULD PROBABLY have let things lapse after his son—the only one with whom he had any relations at all—passed away, but his daughter-in-law had adopted him. "You're all the family I've got left," she told him, and the irony was that he had never really liked her very much in the first place. He'd always thought she was a little empty-headed and gossipy—one of those people who had to manage everything, were always too ready to give advice, or suggest a course of action, or give an outright order. She was fifty-two years old and looked ten years older than that, but she called him Dad, and she had the energy of six people. She came by to see him every day—she seemed to think this was something they'd arranged—and she would go through his house as if it were hers, setting everything in order, she said, so they could relax and talk. Mostly this meant that she would be telling him what she thought he could do to improve his life, as if at eighty-three there were anything much he could do one way or the other.

She thought he spent too much time watching television, that he should be more active; she didn't like his drinking, or the fact that he wasn't eating the healthiest foods; it wasn't right for a person to take such poor care of himself, to be so negligent of his own well-being, and there were matters other than diet or drink that concerned her: the city was dangerous, she said, and he didn't have good locks on his doors or windows; he'd developed bad habits all around; he left the house lights burning through the night; he'd let the dishes go. He never dusted or tidied up enough to suit her. He was unshaven. He needed a haircut. It was like having another wife, he told her, and she took this as praise. She never seemed to hear things as they were meant, and it was clear that in her mind she was being quite wonderful—cheerful and sweet and witty in the face of his irascibility and pigheadedness. She said he was entitled to some measure of ill temper, having lived so long; and she took everything he said and did with a kind of proprietary irony, as if another person were there to note how unmanageable and troublesome he could be. At times it seemed that any moment she might turn and speak to some unseen auditor: "You see, don't you? You see what I have to go through with this guy?"

He had never considered himself to be the type of man who liked to hurt other people's feelings, but he was getting truly tired of all this, and he was thinking of telling her so in terms that would make her understand he meant business.

Lately, it had been the fact that he was living alone. There was a retirement community right down the street: a room of his own; games, movies, company, trips to other cities, book clubs, hobbies, someone to get the meals. She went on and on about it, and Theodore would close his eyes and clap his hands over his ears and recite Keats, loudly, so he couldn't hear her. " 'My head aches, and a drousy numbness pains my sense,' " he would shout, " 'As though of hemlock I had drunk.' As though of hemlock, Judy. Hemlock, get it? Hemlock."

"All right," she would say, "All right, all right," and she would move about the house picking things up and putting them down, her mouth set in a determined straight line.

But of course there was always the next round, and when her temper had cooled she seemed to enjoy getting back into it— she hadn't spent a lifetime telling other people what to do without having developed a certain species of hope or confidence in her ability to bend someone else's will to her own. He had watched her lead her husband around like a puppy most of his poor, cut-short life, and he told her so.

"John was happy with me, which is more than I can say for his mother when she was with you," she said. "He had a good, rich, full life."

"Sixty-six years is not a rich full life in my book."

"No, it wouldn't be, in your book."

"Maybe Margaret wasn't happy with me because I wouldn't let her lead me around like a damn puppy dog all the time."

"No, and she wouldn't let you lead her around, either."

"It was twenty years ago—who can remember who led who?"

"Speaking of remembering things, you have two sons still living in Vermont, and time isn't standing still. Don't you think it would be a good thing for you to reopen lines of communication? Maybe get on a plane and go see them. I thought you might make things up at John's funeral, and I was very sad to see that you didn't. John would've liked it if you had. Why don't you go visit them in their homes—see what their lives are like. They have children you've never seen, wives you haven't met."

"I knew the first wives."

"Is that why they fell from grace? Because they had divorces?"

"They fell from grace, as you put it, because they were messy and selfish about their lives and because they never had a thought for me or their mother."

"Do you know what John thought about the whole thing?"

"I don't care what John thought about the whole thing."

"He thought we stayed in your good graces because we kept everything about ourselves a secret—you never knew what trouble we had."

SHE was a registered nurse specializing in pediatrics, and she was mostly on morning shifts, so he would say he liked that time the best: he would leave the phone off the hook and lie in bed reading the newspapers until his eyes hurt. Then he would get up and fix himself an egg, a piece of toast. By this time the sun would be high. He would pour himself a tumblerful of whiskey and take it out on the front porch to sit in his wicker chair in the warmth and sip the whiskey until it was gone. The sun warmed his skin; the whiskey warmed his bones. Before him was the street, what traffic there was; it all looked as though it moved behind smoked glass. If he was really relaxed, he might doze off. It would be shady now, past noon. He would drift, and dream, and in the dreams he was always doing something quite ordinary, like working in the yard, or sitting in the shade of a porch, dreaming. When he woke up he would have a little more of the whiskey, to get ready, he told himself, for her arrival.

Today he went out back to talk over the fence, as he sometimes did, to his one acquaintance in the neighborhood, who was twenty years his junior, and a very bad hypochondriac. It made him feel good talking to this poor man, so beaten down by his own dire expectations. And it was good to know that Judy wouldn't find him on the porch, half asleep, out of dignity for the day, an old, dozing man. He looked at the mess in the kitchen on his way through, and felt a little rush of glee as if this were part of a game he was winning. His neighbor sat in a lawn chair with a newspaper in his lap; *he* was dozing, and this was how he spent *his* afternoons. Theodore called to him from the fence, and he stirred, walked over. The two of them stood there in the sun talking about the hot weather. When Judy arrived, she sang hello to Theodore from behind the back-door screen and said she would make some iced tea.

Then she said, "I'll get your straw hat, Dad. The sun's so bright!"

"The way she worries about me," Theodore said to his neighbor. "Jesus."

The neighbor said, "I got severe abdominal cramps, lately."

"Pay no attention to it," Theodore said.

"It's quite bad sometimes—it radiates into my shoulder. I'm afraid it's my pancreas."

"What the hell is that?"

"The pancreas is something you have to have or you die."

"Well, then I guess we got ours."

"You mean to tell me you don't know what the pancreas is?"

"Sure, I know what it is," Theodore said, "I just don't think about it a lot. I bet I haven't spent five minutes thinking about my pancreas in my whole life."

"I believe mine hurts," said his neighbor.

"Maybe it hurts because you're thinking about it. Stand around and think about your lungs for a while, maybe it'll go away and your lungs will start to hurt."

"You noticed something funny about my breathing."

"I thought we were talking about your pancreas."

Judy came out of the house, carrying a tray with iced tea on it, and wearing Theodore's wide-brimmed straw hat at a crooked angle. "If you're going to stand out in the sun you ought to have a hat on," she said to him. She put the tray down on the umbrella table and came over and put the hat on his head. Then she opened the gate and invited the neighbor to come have a glass of iced tea. The neighbor, whose name was Benjamin Hawkins, was obviously a little confused at first, since in the five or six years that they had been meeting to talk over this fence neither of the two men had ever suggested that things turn into a full-fledged visit—not at this time of day, just before supper. It just wasn't in their pattern, though sometimes in the evenings they watched baseball together, and once in a while they might stroll down to the corner, to the tavern there, for a beer. Talking over the fence was reserved for those times when one or the other or both of them didn't feel much like doing anything else.

And so the invitation was not a very good idea, and Theodore let Judy know it with a look—though she ignored it and went right on talking to Ben Hawkins about what a nice thing it was to have a cool drink in the shade on a hot summer day. It was as if she were hurrying through everything she said, her voice rising with emphasis, as she took Ben's arm and started him in the direction of the umbrella table. In only a moment, Theodore understood what was happening, for he had turned and he could see that someone, a woman, not young, was standing in the back door.

"Well," Ben was saying, "you make it sound so good, Mrs. Weathers."

"What the hell," Theodore said to his daughter-in-law.

She squeezed his elbow, and asked for kindness. "This is a nice lady I work with sometimes at the hospital. She's a volunteer—and she's a doll."

"I don't remember asking you to introduce me to people."

"Dad—please. She's already nervous about meeting you."

"I don't remember saying a thing about being introduced to anyone."

"She was a mathematics teacher, Dad—like you. And she loves poetry and books. She's a wonderful talker."

"So, put her on Johnny Carson."

"This is what I have to deal with," she said to Ben.

"This is what she has to deal with in my house," Theodore said.

"Dad, I swear I'll never forgive you."

She took Ben by the elbow again, and walked with him across the yard, and Theodore followed, lagging behind. The old woman opened the back door and stepped out on the small porch there, already apologizing for having intruded, speaking so low that you had to strain to hear her, while Judy forged on with the introductions, as if this were the beginning of a party. She hustled and got them all seated at the umbrella table and then she poured the iced tea, and nobody had a thing to say until Ben asked the woman, whose name was Alice Karnes, if she ever had any trouble with caffeine in her system.

"Pardon me?" Alice Karnes said.

"Well, I guess I was wondering if any of us are allergic to caffeine. It does funny things to me—"

"That's your nerves," Judy said.

"I've read that caffeine raises your blood pressure," said Ben. "I only allow myself two cups of coffee a day, and I've had my two cups—so this tea is cheating."

There was a pause in which everyone seemed to consider this, and finally Judy remarked that the tea was decaffeinated. "Oh, well," Ben said, and laughed. Theodore stared off at the fenced yards in their even rows down the block, and left his glass untouched; Judy knew very well that he didn't like sweet drinks. He would have preferred a touch of whiskey, and apparently the thought produced the words, because now Judy had fixed him with her eyes.

"Did I speak out of turn?" he said.

Judy seemed about to scold, but then her guest spoke: "Actually, I think I'd like a touch of whiskey myself."

Theodore looked at her. "What was your name again?"

"I'm Alice Karnes."

"Where you from, Alice."

"Why, I'm from Ohio."

"And I bet they drink good whiskey in Ohio, don't they."

"I never thought about it, but I guess they do."

"Would you like a touch of Virginia bourbon whiskey?"

She looked a trifle uncertain, glancing at Judy. Then she nodded. "I believe I would, yes."

"I never met anybody that a little whiskey wouldn't improve," Theodore said.

"It kills brain cells," said Judy.

"But we have millions of those," Ben Hawkins said.

Theodore had already got to his feet, and was going into the house. He had some of today's bottle left, and since Judy had moved in on his life he kept a stash in the basement, behind a brick in the wall at the base of the stairs, where for thirty-two years he had hid pint bottles of whiskey from his wife, Margaret. Margaret had been a very religious woman with a strong inclination to worry, whose father had stupidly drunk himself into ruin. Theodore had managed to convince her that one drink was all right—was even beneficial—and so he would have his one drink in the evenings, and then if he wanted more (he almost always wanted at least a little bit more) he would sneak it. Margaret had gone to her grave convinced of the moderate habits of her husband, who, often enough in the thirty-two years, came to bed late, and slept more deeply than he ever did when there *was* no inducement to sleep coursing through his blood. In the last few weeks he had gone back to keeping the stash, partly as a defense against the meddling of his daughter-in-law—the idea had come from that—but also, now, because it brought back a sense of his life in better times.

Except that this time of all times, all the thousands of times he'd descended these stairs with the thought of a drink of whiskey . . . this time something gave way in his leg, near the knee.

It might have been simply a false step. But something that had always been there before wasn't there for a crucial, awful instant, and he was airborne, tumbling into the dark. He hit twice, and was conscious enough to hear the terrible clatter he made—his leg snapped as he struck bottom. It sounded like an old stick. Nothing quite hurt yet, though. What he felt more than anything was surprise. He lay there at the bottom of the stairs, still in his straw hat, waiting for someone to get to him, and then the pain began to seep into his leg; it made him nauseous. "Goddamn," he said, or thought he said. Then Judy was on the stairs, thumping partway down. He believed he heard her cry of alarm, and he wanted to tell her to calm down and shut up, a woman more than fifty years old crying and screaming like a little girl. He wanted to tell her to please get someone, and to hurry, but he couldn't speak, couldn't draw in enough air. Somewhere far away Benjamin Hawkins was crying out for God, his voice shaking, seeming to shrink somehow, and

Theodore strained to keep hearing it, feeling himself start downward, floating downward and into some other place, a place none of them could be now. It was quiet, and he knew he was gone, he was aware of it, and he turned in himself and looked at it—a man knocked out and staring at his own unconsciousness. Then it was all confused, he was talking to his sons, it was decades ago—they were gathered around him, like a congregation, and he was speaking to them, only what he was saying made no sense; it was just numbers and theorems and equations, as if this were one of the thousands of math classes he had taught. There had been so many times when he had constructed in his mind exactly what he would say to them if he could have got them together like this—all their slights and their carelessness and their use of him, and their use of their mother, all the things he wanted them to know they had done, and here he was with math coming out of his mouth.

He woke up in a bright hospital room with a television set suspended in the air above his head, and a window to his left looking out on a soot-stained brick wall. Sitting in one of two chairs by his bed was a woman he did not at first remember having seen before.

"Who are *you*," he said.

"Alice Karnes."

He looked along the length of his body. His leg was in an ugly brace, and there was a pin sticking through his knee. It went into the violet, bruised skin there like something stuck through rubber. There were pulleys and gears attached to an apparatus at the foot of the bed, looking like instruments of torture. He lay back and closed his eyes, and remembered his dream of talking, and thought of death. It came to him like a chilly little breath at the base of his neck, and he opened his eyes to look at Alice Karnes.

"Does it hurt very bad?" she asked.

"What're you doing here," he said.

"Judy asked me to come. I'm sorry."

"How long have I been here."

"Just a day. I'm sorry—last night and today."

"What is Judy doing?"

"She went to get something to eat. She wanted me to stay in case you woke up. You've been in and out, sort of."

"I don't remember a thing." He looked at her. She had very light blue eyes, a small, thin mouth. Her hair was arranged in a tight little bun on top of her head. She sat there with her hands folded tightly in her lap, smiling at him as if someone had just said something embarrassing or off-color. "What're we supposed to do now," he said.

"Well, I don't think we'll do any calisthenics," she said. Then she blushed. "I guess that's a bad joke, isn't it."

"It's hilarious. I'm chuckling on the inside."

"I'm sorry."

"You're trying to be kind, is that it?"

"Judy didn't want you to wake up alone—"

"Maybe I want to be alone."

"That's your privilege." She sat there.

"And what do *you* want?"

"Oh, I wouldn't be able to say."

"Why not?"

She shrugged. "Judy wanted me to sit with her. I felt bad about what happened to you."

"I've never been in a hospital as a patient in my life," he said. "Not in eighty-three years."

"I guess there's a time for everything."

"I guess there is."

"Do you want me to leave?" she asked him.

He had closed his eyes again. It had come to him that he might never leave the hospital. He breathed slowly, feeling himself begin to shake deep in his bones.

"Of course, I don't mind staying," she said.

"Why?" His voice had been steady; he'd heard how steady it was.

"I'm the volunteer type," she said.

"I don't want any damned charity," he said, trying to glare at her.

"Oh, it's not charity."

"Charity begins at home. Go home and give it to your own people."

She said something about distances, and times; other lives. He didn't quite catch it. A sudden pain had throbbed through his knee, on up the thigh; it made him realize how badly he'd been hurt, how deep the aches were in his hips and lower back and shoulders. When he touched his own cheek, he felt a lump as big as an ice cube, and it was a moment before he realized that it was a bandage over a bruise or laceration.

"Well, I don't want anything," he heard himself say.

"I'm calling the nurse for you," she said, "Then if you want I'll go."

"Don't go."

"Whatever you say."

"This is awful," he said.

"I'm so sorry," she told him.

"Don't talk to me about sorry. I don't want to hear sorry."

"I'm sorry."

"Jesus."

"I didn't mean that—is there anything I can do to make you more comfortable?"

The pain had let up some, but he was still shaking inside. He took a deep breath. "You could put me out of my misery," he said.

"I've pushed the button for the nurse. She ought to be here."

A moment later, wanting talk, he said "How old are you?"

"Oh, you shouldn't ask a lady her age."

"I'm eighty-three," he said, "goddammit. How old are you?"

"Seventy-eight."

"A baby," he said.

"That's very kind of you."

A moment later, he said, "I remember when I was your age."
She smiled.

"Got any children?" he asked. Then he said, "Come on, talk."

"I had two children—they live in Tennessee—"

"They ever come to see you?"

"I go to see them. Christmases and holidays. And for a while in summer."

The pain had mostly subsided now. He sighed, breathed, tried to remain perfectly still for a moment. Then he turned his head and looked straight at her. "Are you lonely?"

"That's not a proper question to ask someone like me."

"You're lonely as hell," he said.

"And you?" she asked, her eyes flashing.

"I don't think about it if I'm allowed not to."

She looked down at her hands.

"I got a daughter-in-law that insists on reminding me of it —and now she's trying to match us up. You know that, don't you?"

"I wish you wouldn't say such things. She told me I'd like you, as a matter of fact—she said you were interesting and that I'd like you. I found the whole thing very embarrassing."

"You found me a little blunt for you—a little rough, maybe."

"Is that the way you see yourself?"

"Suppose it is?"

"It seems to me that if you knew you were being too blunt or rough you'd do something about it."

"Right," he said, "I should remember to be charming. Can I get you anything?"

"Do you want me to leave? Just say so."

He didn't want her to leave; he didn't want to be alone. He said, "Tell me about your children."

"There's not much to tell—*they* have children. I think I need a frame of reference, you know—a—a context." She pulled the edge of her dress down over her knees. "What about you? Tell me about your children."

"My children are mostly gone now. The ones who survive hate me."

"I'm sure that's not so."

"Don't say crap like that when I tell you something," he said, "I'm telling you something. I know what I'm talking about. There's no love lost, you know? Maybe I just don't have anything else to do right now but tell the truth. And to tell you the truth, I never much liked my children. I never had much talent for people in general, if you want to know the truth about it."

"I think I might've gleaned that," she said.

"Well, then," he told her, "Good for you." The pain had come back, this time with a powerful jolt to his chest and abdomen: it felt like a sudden fright, and he turned his head on the pillow, looking at the room. There was another bed, empty, and with the sheets gone. Someone had put a pitcher of water and a glass on the night table. He closed his eyes again, going down in the pain. Somewhere in the middle of it, he was sure, was his death, and knowing this made him want to say something, as if there were matters that must be cleared up before he let go. But when he searched his mind there was nothing.

"Where is everybody," he said.

"I've been ringing for the nurse. Do you want me to go get one?"

"No. Stay."

"I think that's the first friendly thing you've said."

"Pay no attention to it," he said.

"It was a slip of the tongue?" she asked.

"Exactly."

"I'll disregard it, then."

"Do."

She smiled. "I don't think you're as mean as you think you are."

"I'm dying," he said.

"You have a broken leg, some cuts and bruises."

"I'll probably never get out of this bed."

"You're mind's made up," she said.

"Don't be cute. I hate that—do me a favor and don't be the life-affirming visitor with me, okay?"

"Your mind *is* made up, isn't it?"

They were quiet. A doctor came in and looked into his eyes with a bright light, and touched his knee where the metal pin went in. The doctor was very young and blond and his hair was blow-dried, his nails perfectly manicured. He introduced himself as Doctor German or Garman or something; Theodore wasn't listening. The doctor was a kid, no more than thirty. He smelled like rubbing alcohol and he sounded like somebody doing a television quiz show when he talked, his voice lilting like that, full of empty good cheer and smiles. When he was gone, Alice Karnes said "You can see how alarmed the young man is at your condition."

"What does he care?"

"He's obviously certain you'll never get up."

"I don't need sarcasm now either, thank you."

"Poor man," she said.

He said nothing for a moment, and then the aching in his bones brought a moan up out of him.

"I *am* sorry," she said.

"Sorry for what."

"For being sarcastic."

"I can't figure out what you're doing here at all."

"I asked if you wanted me to leave."

"Yes, you did—and I said no. I remember that clearly. But I still don't know what you're doing here in the first place."

"Well it certainly isn't for romance, is it."

"Why not?" he said. "Let's have a whirlwind courtship."

"I don't drink whiskey," she told him.

He looked at her.

"I don't—I've never even tasted whiskey," she said. "I asked for whiskey, remember? You went in to get it and this happened —and I don't even drink it. I was just trying to be—friendly, I guess."

He stared at her.

"We—we were always very strict Baptists. We never did anything like drinking alcohol—especially whiskey."

"You—" he began.

"I feel responsible," she said.

A nurse came into the room—a woman not much younger than they were. She took his temperature and his pulse and blood pressure, and then she, too, touched his knee where the pin was.

"Nurse," he said, "give me something for the pain."

She put some cold solution on the skin around the opening in the knee, using a Q-tip.

"Nurse."

She looked at her watch. "I'm afraid you're not due for another hour." Her voice was grandmotherly and sweet, and she put her hand on his forehead and smoothed the thin hair back; her fingers were cool and dry.

When Theodore moaned, Alice Karnes said, "Can't you do something for him?"

"We're doing everything we can, Mrs. Weathers." The nurse studied Theodore and then nodded. "Just hold on for another fifteen minutes or so and we'll cheat a little—how's that?"

"What's fifteen minutes, for God's sake," Theodore said, "I'm dying here."

"Just fifteen minutes," the nurse said, turning. She walked out of the room without a word or gesture of leave-taking, as if she had been in the room alone.

"Did you hear what she called me?" Alice Karnes said.

He couldn't think. He said, "Tell me."

"She called me Mrs. Weathers."

"She did, did she?"

"The assumptions people make."

"Maybe we could kill her for it," Theodore said.

She smiled at this, and then she reached over and put her hand on his arm. For a long moment she left it there, without saying anything, and then she took it away, sat back, still smiling.

"Well," he said.

She said, "Try to sleep now."

"You got me all excited," he said.

Her smile changed slightly, and she looked away out the window.

HE was in the hospital for almost a month. They put his leg in a cast, and they showed him how to use crutches, and they all talked about how strong he was, a man who ought to live to be a hundred and twenty; they congratulated him for his quick adjustment to the new situation. They showed him why he would always have to use a cane. They laughed at his ill temper and his gruff ways and his jokes, and when they sent him home a group of the nurses and therapists chipped in and bought him a large basket of fruit and a card with a picture of the Phantom of the Opera on the front of it and an inscription that read, "Why did she turn away when I tried to kiss her?" The card was signed by everyone, including the young blond doctor, Doctor Garman— who called him Dad, just as Judy did, with the same proprietary irony. He didn't mind, particularly. He was just glad to be going home. Judy had come to see him almost every day, and he made jokes about having nothing to put between himself and her except feigned sleep. She brought Alice Karnes along with her now and then, but rarely left them alone. In Judy's presence, the older woman was often too mortified to speak: Judy kept talking at and through her, obviously trying to get Theodore to see her many fine qualities—how resourceful she was, and self-reliant; how good her stories were and how well she told them; her wit and her generosity and what good friends they had become. The whole thing was like a talk show, except the unfortunate guest never got to really speak for herself.

"You should hear Alice do Keats," Judy said. "She's got you beat, Dad. She knows all of Keats."

"Well," Alice said, "one pocm."

"Yes, but every word of it, and it's a long poem."

"I took a speech class," Alice said. "It's nothing. Everybody had to do it."

"Go ahead, give it to us," Judy said.

"Oh—now, you don't want to hear that."

"We do—don't we, Dad."

Alice looked at Theodore. "Your daughter-in-law just mentioned that you liked to recite Keats aloud, and I told her I knew the one poem."

"Did she tell you just when and how I recite Keats?"

Judy said, "We want to hear you recite your poem, Alice."

"Sure, why not?" Theodore said. He lay there and listened to Alice try to remember the "Ode on a Grecian Urn," her face crimson with embarrassment. It was interesting to watch her thin lips frame the words, and in fact she had a very pleasant voice. He caught himself wondering if Alice Karnes, for all her apparent unease, hadn't planned everything out with Judy. Once, in the first week of his stay in the hospital, he had awakened to find the two of them whispering to each other on the other side of the room; it was clear that something was in contention between them, until Judy saw that he was awake, and immediately changed her demeanor as though to warn the other woman that they were being watched.

Before he got out of the hospital he decided that they were in fact conspiring together about something—they had, after all, become friends, as Judy put it. They were more like sisters, in fact. It was evident enough that Judy wanted to see a romance develop, and Theodore found that he rather liked the idea that the two women were in cahoots about it; it flattered him, of course. But there was something else, too—some element of pleasure in simply divining what they were up to. He felt oddly as if in his recent suffering there had been a sharpening of his senses somehow, as though a new kind of apprehension were possible that hadn't been possible before. He might have expressed it in this way if he'd wanted anyone to know about it. The good thing was that no one did: to Judy he was, of course, the same. He gave the same cantankerous or sarcastic answers to her questions, made the same faces at her, the same mugged expressions; he even continued to recite Keats over her talk when he was tired of listening to her, and he still insisted on his whiskey and his bad habits, though of course, under the circumstances, he had to insist on these things in theory.

But now he was going home. He could get around, however laboriously, on his own. He was almost eighty-four and he had suffered a bad fall, and he was strong enough, after three and a half weeks, to get around on crutches. Of this he was very proud. When Judy came to the hospital to take him home, she naturally brought Alice along, and as the three of them worked together to get him safely into the car, he had a bad moment of remembering the little chilly puff of air he had felt on the base of his neck when he'd first awakened in the hospital bed; he was convinced now that it had been death. He tried to put it out of his mind, but it left its cold little residue, and he was abruptly quite irritable. When Alice Karnes reached into the car to put his shirt collar down—it had come up as he settled himself in the front seat—he took her wrist and said, as roughly as he could, "I'll get it."

"Of course," she said softly.

He sat with his arms folded, hunched down in the seat. He didn't want their talk now or their cheerfulness, their hopes for him. When Judy started the car up he turned to her and said, "I don't want any company today."

"You're going to have it today," she said, as if she were proud of him, "you old goat."

They said nothing all the way to the house. Alice Karnes sat in the back seat and stared out the window. The few times that Theodore looked at her, he felt again the sense of a new nerve of perception, except that it all seemed to bend itself into the shape of this aggravation—as though he could read her thoughts, and each thought irritated him further.

At home, they showed him how they'd fixed everything up for him; they'd waxed the floors and organized the books; they'd washed all the curtains and dusted and cleaned, and everything looked new or bleached or worn away with scrubbing.

"Look here," Judy said, and showed him a half-gallon of bourbon that they had set into the bookcase, like a bookend. "But you can't have any of it now. Not while you're on the antibiotics."

He went out onto the porch to sit in his wicker chair in what was left of the morning's sun there. They helped him. Judy got him a hassock to rest his leg on. It took a long time getting him settled, and they bustled around him, nervous for his unsteadiness. But he was sure of himself. He sat in the chair and took a deep breath, and they stood on either side of him. "Don't loom over me," he said.

Alice Karnes went back into the house.

"There's a new element to your bad temper, Dad. A meanness. And I don't like it."

"I don't know what you're talking about," he said. "You're in my sun."

"I know," said his daughter-in-law, "you just want to be left alone."

Ben Hawkins came walking around the house and up onto the porch. "I saw the car come down the block," he said. "I was watching for you."

"You found me," Theodore said.

"You look okay," said Ben.

"I'm fine."

"He's been such a dear," Judy said, and turned to go back into the house. Ben Hawkins offered a polite bow, which she didn't see, then settled himself into the chair next to Theodore's. He sat there quietly.

"Well," Theodore said.

The other man stirred, almost as if startled. "Yes, sir," he said, "I guess you made it through all right."

"I guess I did," Theodore said.

"I been getting some palpitations, but other than that, okay."

"Palpitations," Theodore said.

"Heart—you know."

"But nothing serious."

"Oh, no. Other than that, okay."

"You been to a doctor?"

"They don't know what they're looking at. I looked it up, though—palpitations are almost always okay."

"There's machines that measure the heartbeat and everything," Theodore said.

"Other than a little palpitation now and then I'm okay, though."

"You'll probably die, don't you think, Ben? It's a distinct possibility, isn't it?"

"I'm feeling better," Ben said.

They were quiet. After a while they exchanged a few remarks about the brightness of the sun, the coolness of the air when the wind stirred. The women came back out, and Ben Hawkins stood up and bowed to them and, after shaking Theodore's hand, took his leave. He went down the steps and walked back around the house, and once again the two women were with Theodore there on the porch. The sunlight had traversed that side of the house; they were in the shade now. It was cool, and quiet. Theodore had watched Ben Hawkins walk away, and the sun had caught a wisp of the man's sparse hair, had shown Theodore somehow the defeat and bafflement in his stride—in the way his back was bent and in the bowed slant of his head.

Theodore had seen it, and his newfound acuity had without warning presented him with a sense of having failed the other man. He tried to reject it, but it blew through him like a soul, and then it opened wide, fanning out in him, such an abysmal feeling of utter dereliction that he gripped the arms of the wicker chair as if to keep from being swept away. And now Judy was talking to him again, telling him about some prior arrangements.

"What?" he said into her talk. "What?"

Alice Karnes had again gone back into the house.

Judy was talking. "I said I got Alice to agree to stay here with you while I go to work, although God knows we ought to just let you fend for yourself—but she still feels bad about your fall. So you are going to let her stay here until I come back from work."

He nodded.

"She's been very kind to you," Judy said, "So please. Remember your manners."

"Yes," Theodore said, not really hearing himself. "Yes."

He watched her walk off the porch and out to her car. She waved, before she drove off, and he held his hand up; but she was waving at Alice, who stood in the doorway behind him, and now cleared her throat as if to announce her presence.

Theodore said, "Well, you going to stand there all day?"

"I thought you might want to be alone," she said.

He heard himself say, "No." Then, "Do you need an invitation?"

He breathed, and breathed again. Judy had driven herself away, and now he felt her absence with something like grief. He couldn't believe it. Alice Karnes stepped out and took the rocking chair across from him. She rested one arm on the porch rail and looked out at the yard.

"I'm only staying as long as Judy continues to feel she needs me," she said.

"You want something to drink?" Theodore managed.

She leaned back and closed her eyes, and breathed a sigh. The sunlight was on her hair, and she looked younger. "I'll fix you something cold," she said.

"Anything," said Theodore.

But they sat there in the shade of the porch. They looked like a couple long married, still in the habit of love.

POLICE
DREAMS

FOR THOMAS PHILION

About a month before Jean left him, Casey dreamed he was sitting in the old Maverick with her and the two boys, Rodney and Michael. The boys were in back, and they were being loud, and yet Casey felt alone with his wife; it was a friendly feeling, having her there next to him in the old car, the car they'd dated in. It seemed quite normal that they should all be sitting in this car which was sold two years before Michael, who is seven years old, was born. It was quite dark, quite late. The street they were on shimmered with rain. A light was blinking nearby, at an intersection, making a haze through which someone or something moved. Things shifted, and all the warm feeling was gone; Casey tried to press the gas pedal, and couldn't, and it seemed quite logical that he couldn't. And men were opening the doors of the car. They came in on both sides. It was clear that they were going to start killing; they were just going to go ahead and kill everyone.

He woke from this dream, shaking, and lay there in the dark imagining noises in the house, intruders. Finally he made himself get up and go check things out, looking in all the closets downstairs, making sure all the doors and windows were secure. For a cold minute he peered out at the moon on the lawn, crouching by the living-room window. The whole thing was absurd: he had dreamed something awful and it was making him see and hear things. He went into the kitchen and poured himself a glass of milk, drank it down, then took a couple of gulps of water. In the boys' room, he made sure their blankets were over them; he kissed each of them on the cheek, and placed his hand for a moment (big and warm, he liked to think) across each boy's shoulder blades. Then he went back into the bedroom and lay down and looked at the clock radio beyond the curving shadow of Jean's shoulder. It was five forty-five A.M., and here he was, the father of two boys, a daddy, and he wished his own father were in the house. He closed his eyes, but knew he wouldn't sleep. What he wanted to do was reach over and kiss Jean out of sleep, but she had gone to bed with a bad anxiety attack, and she always woke up depressed afterward. There was something she had to work out; she needed his understanding. So he lay there and watched the light come, trying to understand everything, and still feeling in his nerves the nightmare he'd had. After a while, Jean stirred, reached over and turned the clock radio off before the music came on. She sat up, looked at the room as if to decide about whose it was, then got out of the bed. "Casey," she said.

"I'm up," he told her.

"Don't just say 'I'm up.'"

"I am up," Casey said, "I've been up since five forty-five."

"Well, good. Get *up* up."

He had to wake the boys and supervise their preparations for school, while Jean put her makeup on and got breakfast. Everybody had to be out the door by eight o'clock. Casey was still feeling the chill of what he had dreamed, and he put his hands up to his mouth and breathed the warmth. His stomach ached a little; he thought he might be coming down with the flu.

"Guess what I just dreamed," he said. "A truly awful thing. I mean a thing so scary—"

"I don't want to hear it, Casey."

"We were all in the old Maverick," he said.

"Please. I said no—now, I mean *no*, goddammit."

"Somebody was going to destroy us. Our family."

"I'm not listening, Casey."

"All right," he said. Then he tried a smile. "How about a kiss?"

She bent down and touched his forehead with her lips.

"That's a reception-line kiss," he said. "That's the kiss you save for when they're about to close the coffin lid on me."

"God," she said, "you are positively the most morbid human being in this world."

"I was just teasing," he said.

"What about your dream that somebody is destroying us all. Were you teasing about that too?" She was bringing what she would wear out of the closet. Each morning she would lay it all out on the bed before she put anything on, and then she would stand gazing at it for a moment, as if at a version of herself.

"I wasn't teasing about the dream," he said, "I had it, all right."

"You're still lying there," she said.

"I'll get up."

"Do."

"Are you all right?"

"Casey, do you have any idea how many times a day you ask that question? Get the boys up or I will not be all right."

He went into the boys' room and nudged and tickled and kissed them awake. Their names were spelled out in wooden letters across the headboards of their beds, except that Rodney, the younger of the two, had some time ago pulled the *R* down from his headboard. Because of this, Casey and Michael called him Odney. "Wake up, Odney," Casey murmured, kissing the boy's ear. "Odney, Odney, Odney." Rodney looked at him and then closed his eyes. So he stepped across the cluttered space between the two beds, to Michael, who also opened his eyes and closed them.

"I saw you," Casey said.

"It's a dream," said Michael.

Casey sat down on the edge of the bed and put his hand on the boy's chest. "Another day. Another *school* day."

"I don't want to," Michael said. "Can't we stay home today?"

"Come on. Rise and shine."

Rodney pretended to snore.

"Odney's snoring," Michael said.

Casey looked over at Rodney, who at five years old still had the plump, rounded features of a baby; and for a small, blind moment he was on the verge of tears. "Time to get up," he said, and his voice left him.

"Let's stop Odney's snoring," Michael said.

Casey carried him over to Rodney's bed, and they wrestled with Rodney, who tried to burrow under his blankets. "Odney," Casey said, "where's Odney. Where did he go?"

Rodney called for his mother, laughing, and so his father let him squirm out of the bed and run, and pretended to chase him. Jean was in the kitchen, setting bowls out, and boxes of cereal. "Casey," she said, "we don't have time for this." She sang it at him as she picked Rodney up and hugged him and carried him back into his room. "Now, get ready to go, Rodney, or Mommy won't be your protector when Daddy and Michael want to tease you."

"Blackmail," Casey said, delighted, following her into the kitchen. "Unadulterated blackmail."

"Casey, really," she said.

He put his arms around her. She stood quite still and let him kiss her on the side of the face. "I'll get them going," he said. "Okay?"

"Yes," she said, "okay."

He let go of her and she turned away, seemed already to have forgotten him. He had a sense of having badly misread her. "Jean?" he said.

"Oh, Casey, will you *please* get busy."

He went in and got the boys going. He was a little short with

them both. There was just enough irritation in his voice for
them to notice and grow quiet. They got themselves dressed
and he brushed Rodney's hair, straightened his collar, while
Michael made the beds. They all walked into the kitchen and
sat at their places without speaking. Jean had poured cereal and
milk, and made toast. She sat eating her cereal and reading the
back of the cereal box.

"All ready," Casey said.

She nodded at him. "I called Dana and told her I'd probably
be late."

"You're not going to be late."

"I don't want to have to worry about it. They're putting that
tarry stuff down on the roads today, remember? I'm going to
miss it. I'm going to go around the long way."

"Okay. But it's not us making you late."

"I didn't say it was, Casey."

"I don't want toast," Rodney said.

"Eat your toast," said Jean.

"I don't like it."

"Last week you loved toast."

"Nu-*uh.*"

"Eat the toast, Rodney, or I'll spank you."

Michael said, "Really, Mom. He doesn't like toast."

"Eat the toast," Casey said. "Both of you. And Michael, you
mind your own business."

Then they were all quiet. Outside, an already gray sky
seemed to grow darker. The light above the kitchen table
looked meager; it might even have flickered, and for a bad
minute Casey felt the nightmare along his spine, as if the whole
morning were something presented to him in the helplessness
of sleep.

HE used to think that one day he would look back on these years
as the happiest time, frantic as things were: he and Jean would

wonder how they'd got through it; Michael and Rodney, grown up, with children of their own, might listen to the stories and laugh. How each day of the week began with a kind of frantic rush to get everyone out the door on time. How even with two incomes there was never enough money. How time and the space in which to put things was so precious and how each weekend was like a sort of collapse, spent sleeping or watching too much television. And how, when there *was* a little time to relax, they felt in some ways just as frantic about *that,* since it would so soon be gone. Jean was working full time as a dental assistant, cleaning people's teeth and telling them what they already knew, that failure to brush and floss meant gum disease; it amazed her that so many people seemed to think no real effort or care was needed. The whole world looked lazy, negligent, to her. And then she would come home to all the things she lacked energy for. Casey, who spent his day in the offices of the Point Royal Ballet company, worrying about grants, donations, ticket sales, and promotions, would do the cooking. It was what relaxed him. Even on those days when he had to work into the evening hours—nights when the company was performing or when there was a special promotion—he liked to cook something when he got home. When Michael was a baby, Jean would sometimes get a baby-sitter for him and take the train into town on the night of a performance. Casey would meet her at the station, which was only a block away from the Hall. They would have dinner together and then they would go to the ballet.

Once, after a performance, as they were leaving the Hall, Jean turned to him and said "You know something? You know where we are? We're where they all end up—you know, the lovers in the movies. When everything works out and they get together at the end—they're headed to where we are now."

"The ballet?" he said.

"No, no, no, no, no. Married. And having babies. That. Trying to keep everything together and make ends meet, and going to the ballet and having a baby-sitter. Get it? This is where they all want to go in those movies."

He took in a deep breath of air. "We're at happily ever after, is what you're saying."

She laughed. "Casey, if only everyone was as happy as you are. I think I was complaining."

"We're smack-dab in the middle of happily ever after," Casey said, and she laughed again. They walked on, satisfied. There was snow in the street, and she put her arm in his, tucked her chin under her scarf.

"Dear, good old Casey," she said. "We don't have to go to work in the morning, and we have a little baby at home, and we're going to go there now and make love—what more could anyone ask for."

A moment later, Casey said, "Happy?"

She stopped. "Don't ask me that all the time. Can't you tell if I'm happy or not?"

"I like to hear you say you are," said Casey, "that's all."

"Well, I *are*. Now, walk." She pulled him, laughing, along the slippery sidewalk.

SOMETIMES, now that she's gone, he thinks of that night, and wonders what could ever have been going on in her mind. He wonders how she remembers that night, if she thinks about it at all. It's hard to believe the marriage is over, because nothing has been settled or established; something got under his wife's skin, something changed for her, and she had to get off on her own to figure it all out.

He had other dreams before she left, and their similarity to the first one seemed almost occult to him. In one, he and Jean and the boys were walking along a quiet, tree-shaded road; the shade grew darker, there was another intersection. Somehow they had entered a congested city street. Tenements marched up hill to the same misty nimbus of light. Casey recognized it, and the shift took place; a disturbance, the sudden pathology of the city—gunshots, shouts. A shadow-figure arrived in a rusted-out truck and offered them a ride. The engine raced, and Casey tried to shield his family with his body. There was just the engine at his back, and then a voice whispered "Which of you wants it first?"

"A horrible dream," he said to Jean. "It keeps coming at me in different guises."

"We can't both be losing our minds," Jean said. She couldn't sleep nights. She would gladly take his nightmares if she could just sleep.

ON the morning of the day she left, he woke to find her sitting at her dressing table, staring at herself. "Honey?" he said.

"Go back to sleep," she said. "I woke the boys. It's early."

He watched her for a moment. She wasn't doing anything. She simply stared. It was as if she saw something in the mirror. "Jean," he said, and she looked at him exactly the same way she had been looking at the mirror. He said, "Why don't we go to the performance tonight?"

"I'm too tired by that time of day," she said. Then she looked down and muttered, "I'm too tired right now."

The boys were playing in their room. In the next few minutes their play grew louder, and then they were fighting. Michael screamed; Rodney had hit him over the head with a toy fire engine. It was a metal toy, and Michael sat bleeding in the middle of the bedroom floor. Both boys were crying. Casey made Michael stand, and located the cut on his scalp. Jean had come with napkins and the hydrogen peroxide. She was very pale, all the color gone from her lips. "I'll do it," she said when Casey tried to help. "Get Rodney out of here."

He took Rodney by the hand and walked him into the living room. Rodney still held the toy fire engine, and was still crying. Casey bent down and took the toy, then moved to the sofa and sat down so that his son was facing him, standing between his knees. "Rodney," he said, "listen to me, son." The boy sniffled, and tears ran down his face. "Do you know you could have really hurt him—you could have really hurt your brother?"

"Well, he wouldn't leave me alone."

The fact that the child was unrepentant, even after having looked at his brother's blood, made Casey a little sick to his stomach. "That makes no difference," he said.

Jean came through from the hallway, carrying a bloody napkin. "Is it bad?" he said to her as she went into the kitchen. When she came back, she had a roll of paper towels. "He threw up, for Christ's sake. No, it's not bad. It's just a nick. But there's a lot of blood." She reached down and yanked Rodney away from his father. "Do you know what you did, young man? Do you? Do you?" She shook him. "Well, do you?"

"Hey," Casey said, "take it easy, honey." "Agh," she said, letting go of Rodney, "I can't stand it anymore."

Casey followed her into the bedroom, where she sat at the dressing table and began furiously to brush her hair.

"Jean," he said, "I wish we could talk."

"Oh, Jesus, Casey." She started to cry. "It's not even eight o'clock and we've already had this. It's too early for everything. I get to work and I'm exhausted. I don't even think I can stand it." She put the brush down and looked at herself, crying. "Look at me, would you? I look like death." He put his hands on her shoulders, and then Rodney was in the doorway.

"Mommy," Rodney whined.

Jean closed her eyes and shrieked, "Get out of here!"

Casey took the boy into his room. Michael was sitting on his bed, holding a napkin to his head. There was a little pool of sickness on the floor at his feet. Casey got paper towels and cleaned it up. Michael looked at him with an expression of pain, of injured dignity. Rodney sat next to Michael and folded his small hands in his lap. Both boys were quiet, and it went through Casey's mind that he could teach them something in this moment. But all he could think to say was "No more fighting."

DANA is the wife of the dentist Jean has worked for since before she met Casey. The two women became friends while Dana was the dentist's receptionist. The dentist and his wife live in a large house on twenty acres not far from the city. There's an indoor pool, and there are tennis courts; fireplaces in the bedrooms. There's plenty of space for Jean, who moved in on a Friday afternoon, almost a month ago now. That day she just packed a suitcase; she was simply going to spend a weekend at Dana's, to rest. It was just going to be a little relaxation, a little time away. Just the two days. But then Sunday afternoon she phoned to say she would be staying on through the week.

"You're kidding me," Casey said.

And she began to cry.

"Jean," he said, "for God's sake."

"I'm sorry," she said, crying, "I just need some time."

"Time," he said. "Jean. *Jean.*"

She breathed once, and when she spoke again there was resolution in her voice, a definiteness that made his heart hurt. "I'll be over to pick up a few things tomorrow afternoon."

"Look," he said, "what is this? What about us? What about the boys?"

"I don't think you should let them see me tomorrow. This is hard enough for them."

"*What* is, Jean."

She said nothing. He thought she might've hung up.

"Jean," he said. "Good Christ. Jean."

"Please don't do this," she said.

Casey shouted into the phone. "*You're* saying that to *me!*"

"I'm sorry," she said, and hung up.

He dialed Dana's number, and Dana answered.

"I want to speak to Jean, please."

"I'm sorry, Casey—she doesn't want to talk now."

"Would you—" he began.

"I'll ask her. I'm sorry, Casey."

"Ask her to please come to the phone."

There was a shuffling sound, and he knew Dana was holding her hand over the receiver. Then there was another shuffling, and Dana spoke to him. "I hate to be in the middle of this, Casey, but she doesn't want to talk now."

"Will you please ask her what I did."

"I can't do that. Really. Please, now."

"Just tell her I want—goddammit—I want to know what I did."

There was yet another shuffling sound, only this time Casey could hear Dana's voice, sisterly and exasperated and pleading.

"Dana," he said.

Silence.

"Dana."

And Dana's voice came back, very distraught, almost frightened. "Casey, I've never hung up on anyone in my life. I have a real fear of ever doing anything like that to anyone, but if you cuss at me again I will. I'll hang up on you. Jean isn't going to talk to anyone on the phone tonight. Really, she's not, and I don't see why I have to take the blame for it."

"Dana," he said, "I'm sorry. Tell her I'll be here tomorrow —with her children. Tell her that."

"I'll tell her."

"Goodbye, Dana." He put the receiver down. In the boys' room it was quiet, and he wondered how much they had heard, and—if they had heard enough—how much they had understood.

There was dinner to make, but he was practiced at it, so it offered no difficulty except that he prepared it in the knowledge that his wife was having some sort of nervous breakdown, and was unreachable in a way that made him angry as much as it frightened him. The boys didn't eat the fish he fried, or the potatoes he baked. They had been sneaking cookies all day while he watched football. He couldn't eat either, and so he didn't scold them for their lack of appetite and only reprimanded them mildly for their pilferage.

Shortly after the dinner dishes were done, Michael began to cry. He said he had seen something on TV that made him sad, but he had been watching *The Dukes of Hazzard.*

"My little tenderhearted man," Casey said, putting his arms around the boy.

"Is Mommy at Dana's?" Rodney asked.

"Mommy had to go do something," Casey said.

He put them to bed. He wondered as he tucked them in if he should tell them now that their mother wouldn't be there in the morning. It seemed too much to tell a child before sleep. He stood in their doorway, imagining the shadow he made with the light behind him in the hall, and told them good night. Then he went into the living room and sat staring at the shifting figures on the television screen. Apparently, *The Dukes of Hazzard* was over; he could tell by the music that this was a serious show. A man with a gun chased another man with another gun. It was hard to tell which one was the hero, and Casey began to concentrate. It turned out that both men were gangsters, and Jean, who used to say that she only put TV on sometimes for the voices, the company at night, had just told him that she was not coming home. He turned the gangsters off in mid-chase and stood for a moment, breathing fast. The boys were whispering and talking in the other room.

"Go to sleep in there," he said, keeping his voice steady. "Don't make me have to come in there." He listened. In a little while, he knew, they would begin it all again; they would keep it up until they got sleepy. He turned the television back on, so they wouldn't have to worry that he might hear them, and then he lay back on the sofa, miserable, certain that he would be awake all night. But some time toward the middle of the late movie, he fell asleep and had another dream. It was, really, the same dream: he was with Jean and the kids in a building, and they were looking for a way out; one of the boys opened a door on empty space, and Casey, turning, understood that this place was hundreds of feet above the street; the wind blew at the opening like the wind at the open hatch of an airliner, and someone was approaching from behind them. He woke up, sweating, cold, disoriented, and saw that the TV was off. With a tremendous settling into him of relief, he thought Jean had changed her mind and come home, had turned the TV off and left him there to sleep. But the bedroom was empty. "Jean," he said into the dark, "Honey?" There wasn't anyone there. He turned the light on.

"Daddy, you fell asleep watching television," Michael said from his room.

"Oh," Casey said, "Thanks, son. Can't you sleep?"

"Yeah."

"Well—goodnight, then."

"Night."

So Jean is gone. Casey keeps the house, and the boys. He's told them their mother is away because these things happen; he's told them she needs a little time to herself. He hears Jean's explanations to him in everything he says, and there doesn't seem to be anything else to say. It's as if they were all waiting for her to get better, as if this trouble were something physiological, an illness that deprives them of her as she used to be. Casey talks to her on the phone now and then, and it's always, oddly, as if they had never known anything funny or embarrassing about each other, and yet were both, now, funny and embarrassed. They talk about the boys; they laugh too quickly and they stumble over normal exchanges, like *hello* and *how are you* and *what have you been up to*. Jean has been working longer hours, making overtime from Dana's husband. Since Dana's husband's office is right downstairs, she can go for days without leaving the house if she wants to. She's feeling rested now. The overtime keeps her from thinking too much. Two or three times a week she goes over to the boys' school and spends some time with them; she's been a room mother since Michael started there two years ago, and she still does her part whenever there's something for her to do. She told Casey over the phone that Rodney's teacher seems to have no inkling that anything has changed at home.

Casey said "What *has* changed at home, Jean?"

"Don't be ridiculous," she said.

The boys seem, in fact, to be taking everything in stride, although Casey thinks there's a reticence about them now; he knows they're keeping their feelings mostly to themselves. Once in a while Rodney asks, quite shyly, when Mommy's coming home. Michael shushes him. Michael is being very grown up and understanding. It's as if he were five years older than he is. At night, he reads to Rodney from his Choose-Your-Own-Adventure books. Casey sits in the living room and hears this. And when he has to work late, has to leave them with a baby-sitter, he imagines the baby-sitter hearing it, and feels soothed somehow—almost, somehow, consoled, as if simply to imagine such a scene were to bathe in its warmth: a slightly older boy reading to his brother, the two of them propped on the older brother's bed.

This is what he imagines tonight, the night of the last performance of *Swan Lake,* as he stands in the balcony and watches the Hall fill up. The Hall is sold out. Casey gazes at the crowd and it crosses his mind that all these people are carrying their own scenes, things that have nothing to do with ballet, or polite chatter, or finding a numbered seat. The fact that they all move as quietly and cordially to their places as they do seems miraculous to him. They are all in one situation or another, he thinks, and at that instant he catches sight of Jean; she's standing in the center aisle below him. Dana is with her.

Jean is up on her toes, looking across to the other side of the Hall, where Casey usually sits. She turns slowly, scanning the crowd. It strikes Casey that he knows what her situation is. The crowd of others surges around her. And now Dana, also looking for him, finds him, touches Jean's shoulder and actually points at him. He feels strangely inanimate, and he steps back a little, looks away from them. A moment later, it occurs to him that this is too obviously a snub, so he steps forward again and sees that Dana is alone down there, that Jean is already lost somewhere else in the crowd. Dana is gesturing for him to remain where he is. The orchestra members begin wandering out into the pit and tuning up; there's a scattering of applause. Casey finds a seat near the railing and sits with his hands folded in his lap, waiting. When this section of the balcony begins to fill up, he rises, looks for Dana again, and can't find her. Someone edges past him along the railing, and he moves to the side aisle, against the wall. He sees Jean come in, and watches her come around to where he is.

"I was hoping you'd be here tonight," she says, smiling. She touches his forearm, then leans up and gives him a dry little kiss on the mouth. "I wanted to see you."

"You can see me anytime," he says. He can't help the contentiousness in his voice.

"Casey," she says, "I know this is not the place—it's just that —well, Dana and I were coming to the performance, you know, and I started thinking how unfair I've been to you, and—and it just doesn't seem right."

Casey stands there looking at her.

"Can we talk a little," she says, "outside?"

He follows her up to the exit and out along the corridor to a little alcove leading into the rest rooms. There's a red velvet armchair, which she sits in, then pats her knees exactly as if she expected him to settle into her lap. But she's only smoothing her skirt over her knees, stalling. Casey pulls another chair over and then stands behind it, feeling a dizzy, unfamiliar sense of suffocation. He thinks of swallowing air, pulls his tie loose and breathes.

"Well," she says.

"The performance is going to start any minute," he says.

"I know," she says. "Casey—" She clears her throat, holding the backs of her fingers over her lips. It is a completely uncharacteristic gesture, and he wonders if she might have picked it up from Dana. "Well," she says, "I think we have to come to some sort of agreement about Michael and Rodney. I mean seeing them in school—" She sits back, not looking at him. "You know, and talking on the phone and stuff—I mean that's no good. I mean none of this is any good. Dana and I have been talking about this quite a lot, Casey. And there's no reason, you know, that just because you and I aren't together anymore—that's no reason the kids should have to go without their mother."

"Jean," he says, "what—what—" He sits down. He wants to take her hand.

She says, "I think I ought to have them awhile. A week or two. Dana and I have discussed it, and she's amenable to the idea. There's plenty of room and everything, and pretty soon I'll be—I'll be getting a place." She moves the tip of one finger along the soft surface of the chair arm, then seems to have to fight off tears.

Casey reaches over and takes her hand. "Honey," he says.

She pulls her hand away, quite gently, but with the firmness of someone for whom this affection is embarrassing. "Did you hear me, Casey. I'm getting a place of my own. We have to decide about the kids."

Casey stares at her, watches as she opens her purse and takes out a handkerchief to wipe her eyes. It comes to him very gradually that the orchestra has commenced to play. She seems to notice it too, now. She puts the handkerchief back in her purse and snaps it shut, then seems to gather herself.

"Jean," he says, "for God's sweet sake."

"Oh, come on," she says, her eyes swimming, "you knew this was coming. How could you not know this was coming?"

"I don't believe this," he says. "You come here to tell me this. At my goddamn *job*." His voice has risen almost to a shout.

"Casey," she says.

"Okay," he says, rising. "I know you." It makes no sense. He tries to find something to say to her; he wants to say it all out in an orderly way that will show her. But he stammers. "You're not having a nervous breakdown," he hears himself tell her, and then he repeats it almost as if he were trying to reassure her. "This is really it, then," he goes on. "You're not coming back."

She stands. There's something incredulous in the way she looks at him. She steps away from him, gives him a regretful look.

"Jean, we didn't even have an argument," he says. "I mean, what is this about?"

"Casey, I was so unhappy all the time. Don't you remember anything? Don't you see how it was? And I thought it was because I wasn't a good mother. I didn't even like the sound of their voices. But it was just unhappiness. I see them at school now and I love it. It's not a chore now. I work like a dog all day and I'm not tired. Don't you see? I feel good all the time now and I don't even mind as much when I'm tired or worried."

"Then—" he begins.

"Try to understand, Casey. It was ruining me for everyone in that house. But it's okay now. I'm out of it and it's okay. I'm not dying anymore in those rooms and everything on my nerves and you around every corner—" She stops.

He can't say anything. He's left with the weight of himself, standing there before her. "You know what you sound like," he says. "You sound ridiculous, that's what you sound like." And the ineptness of what he has just said, the stupid, helpless rage of it, produces in him a tottering moment of wanting to put his hands around her neck. The idea comes to him so clearly that his throat constricts, and a fan of heat opens across the back of his head. He holds on to the chair back and seems to hear her say that she'll be in touch, through a lawyer if that will make it easier, about arrangements concerning the children.

He knows it's not cruelty that brought her here to tell him a thing like this, it's cowardice. "I wish there was some other way," she tells him, then turns and walks along the corridor to the stairs and down. He imagines the look she'll give Dana when she gets to her seat; she'll be someone relieved of a situation, glad something's over with.

Back in the balcony, in the dark, he watches the figures leap and stutter and whirl on the stage. And when the performance ends he watches the Hall empty out. The musicians pack their music and instruments; the stage crew dismantles the set. When he finally rises, it's past midnight. Everyone's gone. He makes his way home, and, arriving, doesn't remember driving there. The baby-sitter, a high school girl from up the street, is asleep on the sofa in the living room. He's much later than he said he would be. She hasn't heard him come in, and so he has to try to wake her without frightening her. He has this thought clear in his mind as he watches his hand roughly grasp her shoulder, and hears himself say, loud, "Get up!"

The girl opens her eyes and looks blankly at him, and then she screams. He would never have believed this of himself. She is sitting up now, still not quite awake, her hands flying up to her face. "I didn't mean to scare you," he says, but it's obvious that he did mean to scare her, and while she struggles to get her shoes on, her hands shaking, he counts out the money to pay her. He gives her an extra five dollars, and she thanks him for it in a tone that lets him know it mitigates nothing. When he moves to the door with her, she tells him she'll walk home; it's only up the block. Her every movement expresses her fear of him now. She lets herself out, and Casey stands in his doorway under the porch light and calls after her that he is so very sorry, he hopes she'll forgive him. She goes quickly along the street and is out of sight. Casey stands there and looks at the place where she disappeared. Perhaps a minute goes by. Then he closes the door and walks back through the house, to the boys' room.

Rodney is in Michael's bed with Michael, the two of them sprawled there, arms and legs tangled, blankets knotted and wrapped, the sheet pulled from a corner of the mattress. It's as if this had all been dropped from a great, windy height. Casey kisses his sons, and then gets into Rodney's bed. "Odney," he whispers. He looks over at the shadowy figures in the other bed. The light is still on in the hall, and in the living room. He thinks of turning the lights off, then dreams he does. He walks through the rooms, locking windows and closing doors. In the dream he's blind, can't open his eyes wide enough, can't get any light. He hears sounds. There's an intruder in the house. There are many intruders. He's in the darkest corner, and he can hear them moving toward him. He turns, still trying to get his eyes wide enough to see, only now something has changed: he knows he's dreaming. It comes to him with a rush of power that he's dreaming, and can do anything now, anything he wants to do. He luxuriates in this as he tries to hold on to it, feels how precarious it must be. He takes one step, and then another. He's in control now. He's as quiet as the sound after death. He knows he can begin, and so he begins. He glides through the house. He tracks the intruders down. He is relentless. He destroys them, one by one. He wins. He establishes order.

THE WIFE'S
TALE

J.O. Beale

J.O. Beale is a horse's ass
which anyone can see
he smells like something in the grass

I COULDN'T FINISH THE THOUGHT because I couldn't find the rhyme, though I wrote seven or eight rhyming words in the margin: free, see, be, me. Even don*key*. None of them worked. Finally I scribbled, "He's not my cup of tea." And with that acute sense of failure which is particular only to poets who cannot finish their poems, I put the pencil down and went out into the hall, to the stairs, where I put my arms high over my head, letting the tips of my fingers come together, and did what I dreamed was a singularly graceful pirouette. Then I let my hands fall to my sides and gazed at the front door and the foyer below me. This was the day after my birthday, one week before Christmas—a cold, cold day.

I performed a halfhearted two-step down the stairs, just as my older sister, Laura, had shown me, and Mother called from the living room: "Walk when you use those stairs, Marcie. I don't know how many times I've told you."

But I was already in the foyer. "Yes'm," I said.

Before me was the umbrella stand, Mother's oak cane—from

when her leg was broken—and Laura's baton among the four large black umbrellas there. The cane and the umbrellas were connected in my mind, for the umbrellas had belonged to my father, who had died in the accident that had resulted in Mother's broken leg; I had not been old enough to know or remember any of this, though I think I did have a vague memory of Mother hobbling around on the cane. The baton, Laura's baton, was what I was really looking at that afternoon in the foyer. I had loved watching Laura lead the marchers during the halftimes at the Point Royal High School football games; the baton looked like an electric fan spinning at the end of her arm, and of course, in that majorette's costume, she was quite extraordinarily pretty.

"Marcie?" Mother called now.

"I'm here." I touched the porous metal-gray bulb at the end of the baton, which was just an ornament now, like the umbrellas. The umbrellas were never used because they were made for men, heavy and black like that (or so I thought), and because my father had chosen them for himself. Laura had told me this —Mother, after all these years, and with a daughter growing up ignorant of him, still refused to speak about him. I was always imagining that he must have been quite large, though Laura had told me he was rather small and wiry, not much taller than Mother. But there was a terrible thing about him that I think I knew, somehow, before Laura ever told me (which—lest I seem right off a bit portentous in what is, after all, not a particularly sad or unhappy story—was simply that he had been drunk the night of the accident, and was driving the car when it happened, and was, of course, at fault); the thing Laura actually told me was that he'd had a pretty bad drinking problem, and maybe I put two and two together. At any rate, Laura liked to tell one story about him that I'm not sure I believed, though I would be willing to bet now that it is true. I liked the story, and I used to fight with her to get her to tell it:

"He'd had a little to drink," she said, "eleven o'clock Sunday morning, and he was *drunk.*" (This word, *drunk*, had at that time for us a patina of evil so pervasive that it must have meant *all* forms of evil to us in some magical or incantatory way: it was the last outrage, the total surrender, to be drunk.)

Laura went on:

"Well, he came to church with us. Mother tried to stop him but he came ahead anyway, insisted on driving the car. So we came veering into the church parking lot and he gets out of the car and falls down. We all had to help him up. And then when we got into the church, right in the middle of the priest's sermon, Daddy takes a cigarette out of his shirt pocket and lights it up. I guess he'd forgotten where he was. The priest was going on and on about the sodality or something dull like that, and here's this great cloud of blue smoke wafting to the ceiling from the fourth row. The priest I guess just didn't know what to say or do because there was the longest pause, and then he put his chin on his chest, like this, as if he might belch or something, and said, in the softest little squirrel-like voice, 'Uh, no smoking, sir.' Daddy wrenched himself out of the pew and walked right down the center aisle, eyes straight ahead and that old cigarette cupped in the palm of his hand—oh, Marcie! It was like he was the devil, or something."

LAURA was ten years older than I, and was, as I have said, quite extraordinarily pretty. Everyone remarked on her good looks, her soft dark eyes the color of stormy blue oceans, those legs, the slender hands and wrists, the small waist—tiny and delicate as a doll's, Mother used to say. I had thought she was destined to become a famous entertainer, like Ginger Rogers, whose countenance, in a hundred different photographs and poses, adorned the walls of my room, along with two glossies—my proudest possessions—of Laura in the production of *Vaudeville Follies* put on by Mr. Francis T. Miller at the high school, Mr. Miller being someone who had actually been in vaudeville as a performer, and Laura, of course, being the star of his production. If there was one imperfect thing about my sister, it was her feet, which were a little too long; I don't suppose it's necessary to point out that she was quite sensitive about this ("Boat-feet" I'd call her, and she wouldn't speak for hours), but one doesn't wallow in discouragement when the rest of the world is of the opinion that one's beauty is only marking time, so to speak— that before long such beauty will bring fame and fortune. Now, I'm sure that I exaggerated all of this at the time—I was only nine years old, after all—but in my eyes, at any rate, the golden future was all waiting for my sister, and all she had to do was reach out and grasp it. I, of course, could well imagine that I too would be as fortunate, and when I was alone I liked to pretend that everything had unfolded just as I had dreamed it would.

That afternoon in the foyer, I remember touching the cane end of one of the umbrellas, and imagining it belonged to some great stuffy New York producer, come to sweep Laura and me into an airplane and back to the city with him.

"What're you doing out there?" Mother called.

"Watching for Laura."

"Come in here, honey."

"In a minute," I said. I stepped to the door and pressed my face against one of the panes of glass in it, and stared out at the snow on the row of houses across the street: they seemed coated with sugar, and I thought of the little villages of snow on my birthday cake: Mother's creamy vanilla icing. The sky, though, was all pale ash. I believe I would have said it fit my mood. The night before, during my ninth birthday party—a small affair, just the family and J. O. Beale (whom Laura had invited and who had had the audacity to come, all the way from Richmond) —Laura had announced their engagement. She called me "sourpuss" for the way I took the news, and I had the feeling that it was J. O. Beale who had come up with the word: he, no doubt, thought it—and I—were cute.

It was almost too much to take: Hadn't Laura gone to Richmond, to the academy, to become a dancer? Hadn't that been her fondest wish, her future—our future? We had never once even talked about marriage the way I suppose most ordinary sisters do—we had never considered ourselves ordinary in any sense. That is, not until she brought J.O. into the house.

But he wasn't in the house five minutes before Laura and I were sounding like a pair of husband-hunting sisters out of Jane Austen.

I'd been down with a cold. (Living alone in that big, drafty house with Mother I had begun to learn fear, and the best answer to fear was to get sick and lie down for a day or two: at any rate, that seemed to be the pattern. As for the fear, it was random, it climbed into me and sought any object to fix on: my new vanity mirror with the border of pink light bulbs; Mother's gold-inlaid hairbrush with its few coiled strands of her hair in it; or the filmy, leaded panes of glass in the front door. Often at night I had taken to whining and cuddling my way into Mother's bed for this fear.) But as I was saying, I'd been down with a cold, and was in Mother's bed, and Laura came home with J. O. Beale from South Warren Street, Richmond, and in five minutes we were talking about marriage. She told me she'd met J.O. through the friend of a friend's sister. I listened to this, lying on the bed and watching her primp and smile at Mother's dressing table. J.O., she said, was so shy, and afraid to talk to her, and she'd thought he was the handsomest young man she'd ever seen. In the living room below, Beale and Mother were talking about cough syrup, no doubt, Mother being someone who believed in staying on the subject, and whenever I was sick, of course, I was the subject.

"Don't you want to be a dancer anymore?" I said to Laura.

"Oh, maybe," she answered, turning her head to examine her profile. This preening and mirror gazing seemed like a betrayal of sorts, to me: it was Mother who paid attention to such things. Laura had always been completely at home in her own body, had looked at the world out of those marvelous eyes as unself-consciously as a cat does. And looking at her now, I noticed that her lips were darker.

"You wearing lipstick?" I said.

"Sure."

"I guess you'll *marry* him."

She didn't answer.

"You can't be an entertainer and have a husband," I said.

"He's only visiting, Marcie."

"But you'll marry him. I bet you will."

"Don't you dare say that in front of him." She raised her arms and yawned, then smoothed the front of her blouse, rising slowly, sighing with a satisfaction that I knew had nothing whatever to do with me. "Such silly talk."

I thought of telling her I might die from my illness: I might be so disappointed that I'd lose the will to live if she stopped dancing and got married. But it was just a cold, a runny nose, a phlegmy child's cough, and it's of course hard to think of being very convincing as a tragic figure when one has Vicks VapoRub all over one's chest.

ANYWAY, that afternoon as I stood in the foyer and pressed my face against the glass in the door, I was thinking of all this, like the prophet whose direst predictions have come true, and Mother asked again what I was doing.

"I told you," I said.

"You're too quiet," she said. "It makes me think you're into something. Make a little noise, so I can read in peace. Or come in here with me. They're shopping for a ring, honey, and you don't make an investment like that in a snap. Come in here with me—I'm lonesome."

"In a minute," I said, not too politely.

Stepping back from the window, I watched the smudge of my breathing disappear on the glass. Outside a few snowflakes descended, as if from the eave of the porch. I counted one, two, three. Then there were too many to count. A dog, white as the snow on its back and dirtier than the sky on its underside and legs, trotted past, pausing at the base of the elm tree in our yard, then nosing on out of sight. *J. O. Beale is a dog with dirty fur,* I thought, *a stinker, a jackass and a cur.*

"Marcie, come in here right now, please."

I gave up, and went in to her. She was lying on the sofa with a quilt over her knees, a magazine open in her lap. She liked the ones with the gossip, and the pages of puzzles in back, and on days like this we'd spend hours on one puzzle: she'd figure the answers out and then give me hints until I got them too; and on the rare occasions when I got one first, I would do the same for her. She had worked in the drugstore on the corner since sometime shortly after she got off the cane, and because she was on her feet a lot during working hours, she liked to spend a lot of weekend time on this sofa. And when I was bored with what I could make up to do in my room, or tired of playing with the numberless dull children on our block, I'd come to her and we'd rifle the magazines together.

"I've got a good one here," she said now.

"I don't feel like it," I grumbled, and sat in the easy chair across from her. On the wall above the fireplace, Laura and Mother and I made the lower arc of a circle of framed photographs, the upper part of which was two rectangular gilt-and-glass pictures of Daddy, who seemed to smile at me from every angle, and who seemed to dwarf the hills that were visible in the distance behind him (I am sure now that this is where I'd had the impression of his great size; I don't think I quite understood it then). Laura had said to me once that people in photographs followed one with their smiles the way a bright moon can seem to follow a moving car. I looked at the two faces, both smiling, almost identical, though according to Laura the two pictures were taken years apart.

"Did you nap?" Mother asked. "You were so quiet up there."

"I wrote a poem."

"Oh?"

"It's for Laura."

"Well, isn't that nice."

"I wish you wouldn't patronize me, Mother."

"Well, it is nice. And don't say 'Mother' like that. It's disrespectful."

"It is not disrespectful," I said.

"I don't like the way it sounds, whatever it is, so don't do it."

"Will *he* move in with us?" I asked.

"Do you mean J.O.?"

"Of course."

"Now I don't like the way you say '*he*.' What's the matter with you, anyway? You've been a regular crab all week. Ever since Laura came home. Are you still moping around about her career?"

"Well, it's not fair," I said, "not after the way we planned."

"I've explained this to you, Marcie—things change. People change. You will, too."

We were quiet for a moment.

"I remember how *I* was when I learned I was going to be a bride."

"You make it sound like a disease," I said.

"Well, then—you're not listening to me."

"I heard you."

"Your father actually got down on one knee to ask me."

I said nothing to this because I knew she wouldn't elaborate on it; she'd sigh and go on with her reading, or her puzzle-solving. Hers was an orderly mind: all things in the proper places, including the past: it was all right for the house to be full of mementos of dead years, but one never allowed oneself to really dwell on them—they were talismans of a sort; they offered charms against memory, somehow, or at least against the tricks of memory: it is, isn't it, the thing one stumbles over in the attic that finally deals the harshest blow to the heart. I know all this now, and I believe I sensed it—at least, some of it—then. I looked at the photographs of Daddy, and was abruptly a little uneasy. He had been a *drunk*, and he was dead. Toying with the arm of the chair, thinking about this, I listened to Mother turn the pages of her magazine, and flirted with my uneasiness, as I imagined others must flirt with madness and death.

"Do you want to go out and play?" Mother asked. Her voice startled me.

"I'd catch another cold."

"Suppose so."

"Mother," I said, "I'm sorry, but I don't like J. O. Beale."

"Give him a chance, dear. I don't know why I keep having to tell you that."

"I don't like the way he talks or looks or acts."

"You wouldn't like anyone she brought in here, let's face it. It could be Fred Astaire and you'd thumb your nose." She yawned. It was apparently nothing for her to throw a comment like this in my direction. I pulled a strand of thread out of the chair arm, watched the cloth bunch up: an evil little girl quietly destroying the fabric of a chair in her mother's humble living room.

"I don't like him one bit. I don't like his dirty habits."

"Those are a man's habits, dear. You'll have to get used to them."

"That's a lot of crap," I said.

"Marcie, don't you ever say a word like that again. Not in this house, do you hear?"

"I've heard *him* say it," I said.

"That's his business. Do you understand?"

"Yes, ma'am."

"Now, what do you say?"

"About what?"

"You know very well what."

"I'm sorry."

"That's better."

"But it is a lot of crap," I mumbled.

"What did you say?"

"Nothing."

"You said something—what did you say?"

"I said I don't like him."

She gazed at her magazine.

And I'm not sorry, I thought. Because I hate him. And knowing hatred was a sin, I lay back in the chair reveling in it, gazing at Daddy's picture again. You too, I thought. You too.

"You have to remember," Mother said, "Laura loves him."

"Yes," I said, bitterly.

"And you love Laura, don't you?"

I lay back and closed my eyes; I had never felt quite so confused and weary. The image of the stairs and the tips of my feet dancing at the smooth rounded edges of each step made me open my eyes again. Then I consciously imagined the snowy street and the flakes dropping—a world clean and sure and factual as a photograph. I wondered if I would ever find the energy to live as long as mother had.

"Mother," I said, "when you were my age, what did you want to grow up to be?"

"I think I might have wanted to be a movie star. You know one doesn't have to be very special to want those kinds of things. You're my wonderful darling girl, but you aren't the first to have stars in your eyes."

"I never said I was."

"All the same," she said, "It's nice to know you're not alone."

"Maybe J. O. will have a heart attack," I said.

"Young lady, you get right down on your knees and ask God to forgive you for saying that."

I knelt down in front of the chair and folded my hands as piously as I could, under the circumstances: I was thinking that lots of people had heart attacks.

"What a vile, awful, wicked thing to say."

"I'm praying, Mother," I said, gazing with secret hope at the image of J. O. Beale lying face down in the snow; it was an exact and murderous vision: I even conjured a trickle of blood at the corner of his mouth.

And now the door into the hall opened and Laura's voice came to us, shrill with delight, talking about the snow. Beneath her exclamations was the despised murmur of the still-living J. O. Beale.

"Get up now, quick," Mother said to me, "Sit down."

I obliged, and when Laura came in I managed a reserved smile.

"Lord," she said. "We'll all be buried by tonight." Her hair glistened with melting snow. Oh, she knew how beautiful she was! She was in love! Her every move seemed choreographed to express it: a young woman imbued with the romance of being just exactly what she was. J.O. was behind her, hands confidently in his pockets, the heels of his shoes sounding on the pine floor. Since he was a truck mechanic, I always expected to see grease on him. But there was never a trace—and of course this felt like just one more thing J.O. did to get under my skin. (If it wasn't the sign of some hidden perversion: I had read somewhere that excessively fastidious men were almost invariably hiding some awful truth about themselves.) Now he put his hand on my head. "H'lo, brat."

I shook loose, frowned, settled deep in the chair.

"Mother," Laura said, sitting on the arm of the sofa as if to read the magazine on Mother's upraised knees, "J.O. picked out the most beautiful ring for me. Well"—she smiled coyly at him —"actually, I helped pick it out, didn't I?"

"I can't wait to see it," Mother said.

"Now," J.O. said, "I've got to find a way to pay for it."

"J.O. introduces the vulgar note of money," I said. I was very precocious. He stood over me and told me so.

"Where do you get that stuff?" Mother said to me. "I swear I'm going to start supervising your reading."

"Let's put a fire in the fireplace and snuggle all evening," Laura said.

"Laura," said Mother, "Marcie's written a poem for you."

"It's not finished," I said.

"Come on," J.O. said, "let's hear it."

"As a matter of fact," I said, "it's about you—and I have it memorized."

"Marcie," said Mother.

But it was too late. I thought it would serve them right. I believe I thought that J.O. would be driven from the house by the first line of my poem—not to mention the imperfect and unfinished rest of it. Oh, the power of words! I stood by my chair and, as Mother started to rise from her position on the couch, I fairly shouted: "J. O. Beale is a horse's ass, which anyone can see. He looks like something in the grass . . ." And then, pure as my displeasure and my disappointment, I had my rhyme: "He smells like something in the grass," I shouted, "But he lives up in a tree." I was exultant, standing there under Mother's astonished eyes while Laura bent down, her hand to her lips, moving away from me as if wounded, I thought. J.O. just stood there.

"Marcie . . ." Laura tried to speak. But then she stopped. I looked at J.O., who had now turned and seemed to be waiting only—as I was—to see what would happen next.

What happened next, of course, will not surprise you—but for me then, as I was then, it was the crowning humiliation, the unforgivable crime, the cruel last straw: they laughed. The three of them, in exactly the same instant, like an explosion. I was so aghast at this that I simply sat down in my chair and watched them for a moment.

"Horse's ass," J.O. was saying, still laughing. "What a good one. Horse's ass. Lives in a tree."

I stood. I had had enough. I said "Did you know that our father was a drunk?" I spoke as evenly and as coldly as an old, old, bitter woman.

"Marcie?" my mother said.

"Our father was a drunk," I said again. "He killed himself."

I went past them, out into the hall, to the umbrella stand, and, with a cry that frightened even me, struck Laura's baton against the newel post; it bent almost in two, and I let it fall, turning to face Laura as she appeared in the doorway to the living room.

"Marcie?" she said.

"Leave me alone," I said.

She put her arms around me, and I pulled away. This was impossible to believe: Mother and J.O. were there too, now. They were all concerned; they looked at me with the worried faces of loved ones, of family. And then Laura turned and went up the stairs, gradually breaking into a run, sobbing, moving with such grace and dignity I wanted to cry. Mother followed, or started to, but then there was me to worry about. I removed myself from her attempted embrace and walked back into the living room: what I did not need or want now was pity or concern. I had done something I knew to be spiteful and mean, and although I wasn't in the least repentent about it, I wasn't prepared for these kindnesses in response to it.

I sat in my chair in the living room and wondered, and tried not to cry, feeling my heart constrict with anger. And then J.O. strolled in and stood by the fireplace, looking at Daddy's picture. I glared at him, the cause of all our trouble, thinking about his heartbeat. Casually he turned, crossed the room, his hands folded under his chin. When he stood over me I folded my arms and stared straight ahead.

"I know how you feel," he said.

"It's none of your business," I told him.

"No, I suppose not."

"You leave me alone," I said. "It's none of your affair."

"All the same."

"Why don't you leave," I said.

He leaned down. I smelled tobacco, and what I thought was

grease. Or I wanted it to be grease. I wanted to see tufts of fur on his ears. I had never been this close to him. "What I think you need, little girl, is a good spanking right about now."

"Don't you touch me," I said.

"Oh, I won't touch you. But that is most directly what you need. A whupping. We all need one now and then."

My eyes trailed along his arm to the wall above the mantel, where Daddy smiled benignly at me. I had an awful sense of being too deeply understood. I looked around the room, averting my eyes from him, and then Laura and Mother came back into the room to kneel on either side of the chair and look at me.

I said the only thing I could say. "I'm sorry."

"Upset," Mother was saying, and Laura said something about Daddy.

"May I be excused?" I said into their faces, "I want to go upstairs."

"You go up and lie down, honey," Laura said, "This engagement stuff—and on your birthday—"

"Upsetting," said Mother.

They let me go. I walked out of the room, feeling their eyes on me. I did not look at J.O. again.

"She'll settle down," I heard Mother say.

"I will not," I said to myself as I climbed the stairs. I planned to stay in my room until I died, coming out only to eat a meal or two, or to send away a visitor. I was certain.

And for a long while, that evening, after I had calmed down, I sat in the middle of Mother's bed with my legs crossed, thinking about how I would never, never marry.

CONTRITION

MY SISTER ONLY TOLERATES ME HERE, I'm afraid. She doesn't want to talk about anything much; everything I do is a strain on her. This morning, I wanted to ask if she remembers a photograph of our father. "We used to stare at it and try to imagine him," I say. "I used to carry it around with me—the one Uncle Raymond took with that old box camera of his."

"I don't remember staring at any photograph," she says.

I follow her around the house, talking. I remember that I used to gaze at that one picture, though there were others—there must've been others—trying to imagine myself into the scene, trying to imagine how it must have been on that day when the picture was taken.

"You have Mother's things in the attic, don't you?" I say.

"I don't have the photograph."

"I'm sure Mother would've kept it," I say.

"We'll talk tonight," my sister says. "If you want to talk. But not about any photographs or anything like that. You've got to get up and start again."

"Do you remember the picture exactly?" I say.

"I remember that you've been here a week and haven't had one job interview."

"It's hard for a man my age—a convicted felon."

"Stop it," she says. "Quit bringing it up all the time."

"Maybe I'll go for a walk," I say.

And she says, "We can talk about things tonight."

But at night her husband is there, and while I listen to him talk about the disintegration of the schools (he teaches high school science, and I did too, until I was fired) or listen to him talk about the Yankees, she drafts letters to her two sons, both away at college—the same college, the same dormitory, though one son is two years older than the other and will graduate sooner. If we talk at all, really, it's always about these two—one is letting his grades go to hell playing intramural basketball, the other is in love with a girl who has anorexia and has been in and out of the hospital.

"She's been down to eighty pounds," my sister says. "She doesn't look much heavier than that now. She could be somebody out of those pictures of the death camps. And he says it's because she's depressed. She doesn't like herself. For God's sake."

"I think that's what the doctors are saying about it, though," I say.

"It's ridiculous," my sister says. "We're spending all this money on their education and you'd think somebody would teach them to be a little more careful about who they get involved with."

They're her sons. Her husband is childless, much older than she is; the boys were already out of high school when she met him. He was at George Washington on a summer grant, and she worked as a secretary in the Education Department. They were both recently divorced, and, as my sister put it once, they fell into each other's arms and saved each other. His name is Roger. He's a very kind, quiet, slow-moving man, whose face seems perpetually pinched in thought, as if he's on the verge of recalling something very important. It's always as if he's about to burst into passionate speech. Yet when he actually does speak his voice is high-pitched and timid, and I find myself feeling a little sorry for him.

In the mornings, as he rushes from the house to catch his bus to the high school, my sister hurries along beside him. They talk. She gesticulates and explains; he nods and appears to try to calm her. From time to time one of them glances back at the house, at the window of this room. My sister will explain these little episodes by talking of Roger's forgetfulness. "He forgot his wallet again," she says, "Who does that remind you of?"

"Me?" I say.

"No, you never forgot anything in your life."

"Well, who," I say. "You?"

"Eddie," she says. "Don't you remember how bad Eddie always was?"

Eddie was her first husband, and I don't know why she brings him up to me in this way because I never really knew the man. I left home shortly after she met him. Uncle Raymond had died, and Mother was little more than an invalid. There was ill feeling over my decision to leave, though I did have a job to go to. It wasn't as though I was hiring onto a ship or something, to wander the high seas. It was a very good job which I grew to like very much. But I remember my sister thought I was merely running away and for a long time after I went to teach in New York, I didn't hear from her. In fact, she wrote that first time only to inform me of Mother's death. I had expected the news for some time, because Mother's letters had stopped scolding me about my failure to write my sister, and began to repeat, over and over, her regret about having spoken meanly to my father on the last day he was alive. It was apparently something she'd been carrying around all those years. They had been having some trouble over money, and she called him a weakling. It was the last thing she ever said to him. My wife, who lives in Florida now with someone named Kenny, left me a note which read, simply, *You deserve this.* She knew Kenny from her work; they were telephone friends. Kenny was the Florida representative for Satellite Analysis Systems Corporation, and they used to talk on the phone. When our trouble began, she started confiding in Kenny. Now they live together in a condominium on the Gulf. Kenny used to take drugs, she says, but that's all over now. Lately, I hear from her mostly through her lawyer, whose name is Judith. We're on a first-name basis because Judith used to be *our* lawyer. Everything has been fairly cordial, but they did take the house and most of the things in it; they put it all on auction, and since I no longer had my job, and there wasn't much anyone would say to me where we lived, I came here, and was taken in.

That first night I explained to my sister what had happened, and why I was alone. We were in her car, on the way to Point Royal from the train station. "My principal asked me to find out what I could about the supposed drinking problem of one of the school's assistant principals," I said, "Nothing came of it except that he got wind of it and started working very hard to ruin me with the school board. Then my principal left, and this man replaced him. Life got hard. And *I* started being the one who was drinking. Things went from bad to worse. Janice was already talking about leaving me. I went into the city alone one night, had a few whiskeys, and you know the rest."

"You shouldn't have married her," my sister said.

"We were married for sixteen years," I said.

She was driving, holding the wheel with both hands. "It's so stupid. It's—it's humiliating. I don't want you to tell anyone here anything about it."

"No," I said, "of course. No."

"My God," she said, "What will you do now?"

"I thought of suicide before I called you. Seems I hadn't the courage."

"Suicide. What's happened to you? How could you wind up like this—how could you let it happen?"

"I don't have any explanation," I said.

"Well," she said, "I wish you hadn't come *here* with it all." We were pulling into her driveway. Roger stood out in the porch light, his hair blowing in the chilly night breeze. He looked irritable and tired, but he took the trouble to come down the walk and shake my hand.

"I had no place to go," I said.

"As long as a man has a family, he has a place to go," he said, and my sister gave him a look.

STILL, she allows me to stay, on the condition that I see a counselor at the local clinic. Actually, this is a compromise: she had originally wanted me to see a priest, which was something I just couldn't bring myself to do. There is also the stipulation that I find work as quickly as possible; but the counselor has suggested a couple of weeks' rest. "Everything fell apart," I tell him. "My wife lives with someone named Kenny," I tell him. "I want to tell children about gravity and what happens when it thunders, but I have a criminal record. I took apart a prostitute's poor, shabby room, and broke her arm, and got arrested. I assaulted a police officer. I don't even know how it happened. I'm born Catholic and God is like a hurricane on the West Coast. I never saw my father." He listens and I grow weary of my own voice, my litany. He's like a priest, finally, and I tell him so.

"Of course," he says.

"Just tell me I'm forgiven," I say.

"You're forgiven," he says.

"I don't feel forgiven," I say.

"It takes steady effort for a while," he says. He folds his hands and begins to talk about making friends with one's emotions, and I fold my own hands, as if listening. But my mind wanders. I remember a sign the nuns put on the wall in the classroom where I spent my sixth-grade year: "MY STRENGTH IS AS THE STRENGTH OF TEN BECAUSE MY HEART IS PURE." And I think of the photograph, the one picture of my father, the snapshot about which my sister claims to have no memory of fascination. She's the only person in the picture who isn't dead now. My mother cradles her, smiling into the sun; behind my mother, a little to the side, my father is bending over with his hands on his knees, looking out at us as if waiting for a ball to be thrown, or a signal to be called, some action to begin. At his shoulder, as though he's supporting them, are a beach cottage and the sea.

I ask my sister, "What do you imagine ever happened to it?"

"You're talking about that goddamn picture again," she says. "What could possibly be so important about a picture of somebody you never knew?"

"You remember," I say. "I used to carry it around—Uncle Raymond took it from me. He took it from me and gave it to Mother."

"You've just come here to give up," she says. "Is that it?"

"Do you recall," I say, "when Uncle Raymond took it from me and gave it to Mother and said, 'That's the story of the man's life'?"

"I remember no such thing."

"Do you ever think about Uncle Raymond?"

"Of course. He was like a father to us."

"No," I say, "Not to me. Why did he and Mother have so little to say about Father?"

"I've never bothered myself with that."

"Uncle Raymond was no father to me," I say.

"Stop this," she says. "Get out and find yourself something to do. You can't just stay here indefinitely—we can't be expected to support you much longer if you won't do anything to help yourself."

"I'm trying to," I say.

"And how can you say that about Uncle Raymond? He was a quiet man, he didn't know how to show affection maybe—but he was *there*; he supported us, fed us."

"I always felt starved," I say.

But she doesn't want to talk anymore, complains of not having enough time to herself with me in the house. I come to this room, and sit down to write about Uncle Raymond, who was indeed a quiet man. I remember his white socks, his seafood, his Lucky Tiger hair oil, his Ram's Head Ale, and his camera. I have an image of him sitting in front of a television set—one of the first models General Electric made—watching Milton Berle and listening to H. V. Kaltenborn on the radio: he didn't quite believe in television then, and was afraid he'd miss something. I remember the confusion of noises in the rooms—applause, music, voices, laughter. Uncle Raymond had been in the war in the Pacific, was one of fifteen survivors of a brigade that landed on Tarawa. He was suspicious of the Jews, hated Truman. Listening to the news, he would raise his voice now and again. "That bastard Truman," he would say, or "That goddamn haberdasher." He was the one who took the photograph, using a black box camera his father had given him on his twenty-first birthday. Kodak. All those years he'd kept that camera; it sat like a truncated telephone in the middle of his bureau drawer, the lens broken because he'd dropped it once while trying to change the film. Once I went into his room— it was some time after he'd taken the photograph from me and, holding it up to the light, said to my mother, "You know, that's the story of the man's life." I crept to the bureau while he slept, and lifted the camera to look through the lens. A jagged line separated the magnified from the unmagnified world. Looking at the crucifix on the wall above his bed, I snapped the shutter. Uncle Raymond woke, groaning, sat up suddenly, looking at me and blinking. I put the camera down.

"Get out of here," he said.

"Uncle Raymond," I said, "I dreamed last night that I was a mailman—I was delivering mail."

"What the hell?" He reached for his cigarettes on the night table.

I kept talking because I was in his room and was a little afraid, but also because in fact I *had* been troubled by a nightmare that I was delivering mail, and that everywhere I went the houses were all empty, doors were ajar in the wind, and glass was broken out of windows. I told him only about finding the houses empty.

"Yeah?" he said, "So?"

"It scared me."

"It was a nightmare, then. Nightmares are scary." He lighted a cigarette. He never smoked except in this room, because Mother couldn't stand the smell of tobacco.

"Uncle Raymond, can I have the picture back?" I said.

"What picture? What time is it? What're you doing here anyway?"

"I just want to know what you did with the picture."

"Jesus," my uncle said. "Will you get out of here?"

"What happened to my father?" I said.

He stared at me. I suppose he was trying to wake up. "I don't know what you're trying to do," he said. "You already know about him—he was just like a lot of people. I told you all this before. He was a guy. He liked sports. He played a lot of sports and he was pretty good at them. There isn't anything else."

I stood there with my hands at my sides, waiting.

"All right," he said, "what else do you want?"

"My father wasn't in the war," I said.

"No. He had flat feet. He got to stay home. But he was unlucky—all right? A girder fell in the shipyard where he worked and he was standing under it. And he got killed. He never knew what hit him and he probably died happy. He never worried about anything in his life except the next game of whatever it was he happened to be playing, and he probably died happy. Now, what more can I tell you?"

"Nothing," I said.

ROGER hints about my leaving. He lies back in his easy chair in his clean white shirt, his hands tenderly caressing the loose flesh below his chin. Papers and small pieces of note cards jut from his pockets. My sister is in my room, dusting and cleaning, as if I had already gone.

"You can't just sit still like this," Roger says, "You're a grown man. A lot of men have to start over at your age."

"I don't know where to go," I say. "It's ridiculous, but I want to look at my father again. I feel as though I took nothing at all with me out of my childhood, but surely there's something in all those boxes up in your attic."

"There's nothing of interest to you in my attic," he says.

"There's a photograph," I say.

"I know all that," he says. "I've heard it all over and over again from *her.*" He sits forward in the chair. "I've done my best to be kind, here, but you have to be out by the end of the week. I'm sorry, but that's just the way it's got to be."

"Of course," I say, "I understand."

I think of my father. I lie awake in what may be my last night here, imagining his speed and deftness and bad luck. If I sleep, I may dream he's sitting on a tattered mattress in an upstairs room— a hotel in Point Royal in 1938—drunk, his money spent, his clothes strewn everywhere, while before him, in the meager light of a single lamp, a woman dresses slowly. Say his wife is leaving him. Say he's filled with fear and anger and say the woman is someone he's never met before in his life.

She laughs, softly. "You married?"

My father, in this dream, lies, "No." He thinks of his own father, perhaps, or of his wife. He covers himself, pulls at a piece of his clothing on the floor by the bed. "I feel sick," he says.

"You didn't get nothing done," she says. "Nothing to be sick about."

And say that then the police come in, not charging loudly as one might suppose, but casually, as if browsing in a store: they know the people they will arrest, except for my father, who, in his panic, picks up the lamp by the bed and begins to flail and beat at the policemen and at the woman. Say he breaks the poor woman's arm with the lamp; say he's dragged fighting from the room and the building, and that he knows, even while it's all happening to him, that this is the one truest mistake of his life and that he'll never outlive it.

Lying awake, thinking I may dream this, I hear the wail of a siren, and the soft protesting of the floor beyond the room, where my sister and her husband pace and whisper. I would like to find the photograph. It's a small thing, I know; it changes nothing, but I want to look at my father's face and see if I can find in it some trace of a thing he regrets. I would like to know what that thing is.

Oh, and I would like to start over, all over again, from the very beginning, as if I were new and clean and worthy, and the envy of people like me.

ANCIENT
HISTORY

IN THE CAR ON THE WAY SOUTH, after hours of quiet between them, of only the rattle and static of the radio, she began to talk about growing up so close to Washington: how it was to have all the shrines of Democracy as a part of one's daily idea of home; she had taken it all for granted, of course. "But your father was always a tourist in his own city," she said. "It really excited him. That's why we spent our honeymoon there. Everybody thought we'd got tickets to travel, and we weren't fifteen minutes from home. We checked into the Lafayette Hotel, right across from the White House. The nicest old hotel. I was eighteen years old, and all my heroes were folksingers. Jack Kennedy was President. Lord, it seems so much closer than it is." She was watching the country glide past the window, and so Charles couldn't see her face. He was driving. The road was wet, probably icy in places. On either side were brown, snow-patched hills, and the sky seemed to move like a smoke along the crests. "My God. Charles, I was exactly your age now. Isn't that amazing. Well, I don't suppose you find it so amazing."

"It's amazing, Mom." He smiled at her.

"Yes, well, you wait. Wait till you're my age. You'll see."

A little later, she said, "All the times you and your father and I have been down here, and I still feel like it's been a thousand years."

"It's strange to be coming through when the trees are all

bare," said Charles. Aunt Lois had asked them to come. She didn't want to be alone on Christmas, and she didn't want to travel anymore; she had come north to visit every Christmas for fifteen years, and now that Lawrence was gone she didn't feel there was any reason to put herself through the journey again, certainly not to sit in that house with Charles's mother and pine for some other Christmas. She was going to stay put, and if people wanted to see her, they could come south. "Meaning us," Charles's mother said. And Aunt Lois said, "That's exactly what I meant, Marie. I'm glad you're still quick on the uptake." They were talking on the telephone, but Aunt Lois's voice was so clear and resonant that Charles, sitting across the room from his mother, could hear every word. His mother held the receiver an inch from her ear and looked at him and smiled. They'd go. Aunt Lois was not about to budge. "We do want to see her," Charles's mother said, "and I guess we don't really want to be here for Christmas, do we?"

Charles shook his head no.

"I guess we don't want Christmas to come at all," she said into the phone. Charles heard Aunt Lois say that it was coming anyway, and nothing would stop it. When his mother had hung up, he said, "I don't think I want to go through it anywhere," meaning Christmas.

She said, "We could just stay here and not celebrate it or something. Or we could have a bunch of people over, like we did on Thanksgiving."

"No," Charles said, "let's go."

"I know one thing," she said. "Your father wouldn't want us moping around on his favorite holiday."

"I'm not moping," Charles said.

"Good. Dad wouldn't like it."

It had been four months, and she had weathered her grief, had shown him how strong she was, yet sometimes such a bewildered look came into her eyes. He saw in it something of his own bewilderment: his father had been young and vigorous, his heart had been judged to be strong—and now life seemed so frail and precarious.

Driving south, Charles looked over at his mother and wondered how he would ever be able to let her out of his sight. "Mom," he said, "let's travel somewhere."

"I thought we were doing just that," she said.

"Let's close the house up and go to Europe or someplace."

"We don't have that kind of money; are you kidding? There's money for you to go to school, and that's about it. And you know it, Charles."

"It wouldn't cost that much to go somewhere for a while. There's all kinds of package deals—discounts and special fares —it wouldn't cost that much."

"Why don't *you* go?"

"By myself?"

"Isn't there a friend you'd like to go with—somebody with the money to go?"

"I thought *we'd* go."

"Don't you think I'd get in your way a little? A young man like you, in one of those touring groups with his mother?"

"I thought it might be a good thing," he muttered.

She turned a little on the seat, to face him. "Don't mope, Charles."

"I'm not. I just thought it might be fun to travel together."

"We travel everywhere together these days," she said.

He stared ahead at the road.

"You know," she said after a moment, "I think Aunt Lois was a little surprised that we took her up on her invitation."

"Wouldn't *you* like traveling together?" Charles said.

"I think you should go with somebody else if you go. I'm glad we're taking *this* trip together. I really am. But for me to go on a long trip like that with you—well, it just seems, I don't know, uncalled-for."

"Why uncalled-for?" he asked.

"Let's take one trip at a time," she said.

"Yes, but why uncalled-for?"

"We'll talk about it later." This was her way of curtailing a discussion; she would say, very calmly, as if there were all the time in the world, "We'll talk about it later," and of course her intention was that the issue, whatever its present importance, would be forgotten, the subject would be closed. If it was broached again, she was likely to show impatience and, often, a kind of dismay, as if one had shown very bad manners calling up so much old-hat, so much ancient history.

"I'm not doing anything out of duty," Charles said.

"Who said anything about duty?"

"I just wanted you to know."

"What an odd thing to say."

"Well, you said that about it being uncalled-for."

"I just meant it's not necessary, Charles. Besides, don't you think it's time for you to get on with the business of your own life?"

"I don't see how traveling together is stopping me," he said.

"All right, but I don't want to talk about it now."

"Okay, then."

"Aren't you going a little fast?"

He slowed down.

A few moments later, she said, "You're driving. I guess I shouldn't have said anything."

"I *was* going too fast," he said.

"I'm kind of jumpy, too."

They lapsed into silence. It had begun to rain a little, and Charles turned the windshield wipers on. Other cars, coming by them, threw a muddy spray up from the road.

"Of all things," his mother said, "I really am nervous all of a sudden."

Aunt Lois's house was a little three-bedroom rambler in a row of three-bedroom ramblers just off the interstate. At the end of her block was an overpass sixty feet high, which at the same time each clear winter afternoon blotted out the sun; a wide band of shade stretched across the lawn and the house, and the sidewalk often stayed frozen longer than the rest of the street. Aunt Lois kept a five-pound bag of rock salt in a child's wagon on her small front porch, and in the evenings she would stand there and throw handfuls of it on the walk. Charles's father would tease her about it, as he teased her about everything: her chain-smoking, her love of country music—which she denied vehemently—her fear of growing fat, and her various disasters with men, about which she was apt to hold forth at great length and with very sharp humor, with herself as the butt of the jokes, the bumbling central character.

She stood in the light of her doorway, arms folded tight, and called to them to be careful of ice patches on the walk. There was so much rock salt it crackled under their feet, and Charles thought of the gravel walk they had all traversed following his father's body in the funeral procession, the last time he had seen Aunt Lois. He shivered as he looked at her there now, outlined in the light.

"I swear," she was saying, "I can't believe you actually decided to come."

"Whoops," Charles's mother said, losing her balance slightly. She leaned on his arm as they came up onto the porch. Aunt Lois stood back from the door. Charles couldn't shake the feeling of the long funeral walk, that procession in his mind. He held tight to his mother's elbow as they stepped up through Aunt Lois's door. Her living room was warm, and smelled of cake. There was a fire in the fireplace. The lounge chair his father always sat in was on the other side of the room. Aunt Lois had moved it. Charles saw that the imprint of its legs was still in the nap of the carpet. Aunt Lois was looking at him.

"Well," she said, smiling and looking away. She had put pinecones and sprigs of pine along the mantel. On the sofa the Sunday papers lay scattered. "I was beginning to worry," she said, closing the door. "It's been such a nasty day for driving." She took their coats and hung them in the closet by the front door. She was busying herself, bustling around the room. "Sometimes I think I'd rather drive in snow than rain like this." Finally she looked at Charles. "Don't I get a hug?"

He put his arms around her, felt the thinness of her shoulders. One of the things his father used to say to her was that she couldn't get fat if it was required, and the word *required* had had some other significance for them both, for all the adults. Charles had never fully understood it; it had something to do with when they were all in school. He said "Aunt Lois, you couldn't get fat if it was required."

"Don't," she said, waving a hand in front of her face and blinking. "Lord, boy, you even sound like him."

He said, "We had a smooth trip." There wasn't anything else he could think of. She had moved out of his arms and was embracing his mother. The two women stood there holding tight, and his mother sniffled.

"I'm so glad you're here," Aunt Lois said. "I feel like you've come home."

Charles's mother said, "What smells so good?" and wiped her eyes with the gloved backs of her hands.

"I made spice cake. Or I *tried* spice cake. I burned it, of course."

"It smells good," Charles said.

"It does," said his mother.

Aunt Lois said, "I hope you like it *very* brown." And then they were at a loss for something else to say. Charles looked at the empty lounge chair, and Aunt Lois turned and busied herself with the clutter of newspapers on the sofa. "I'll just get this out of the way," she said.

"I've got to get the suitcases out of the trunk," Charles said.

They hadn't heard him. Aunt Lois was stacking the newspapers, and his mother strolled about the room like a daydreaming tourist in a museum. He let himself out and walked to the car, feeling the cold, and the aches and stiffnesses of having driven all day. It was misting now, and a wind was blowing. Cars and trucks rumbled by on the overpass, their headlights fanning out into the fog. He stood and watched them go by, and quite suddenly he did not want to be here. In the house, in the warm light of the window, his mother and Aunt Lois moved, already arranging things, already settling themselves for what would be the pattern of the next few days; and Charles, fumbling with the car keys in the dark, feeling the mist on the back of his neck, had the disquieting sense that he had come to the wrong place. The other houses, shrouded in darkness, with only one winking blue light in the window of the farthest one, seemed alien and unfriendly somehow. "Aw, Dad," he said under his breath.

As he got the trunk open, Aunt Lois came out and made her way to him, moving very slowly, her arms out for balance. She had put on an outlandish pair of floppy yellow boots, and her flannel bathrobe collar jutted above the collar of her raincoat. "Marie seems none the worse for wear," she said to him. "How are you two getting along?"

"We had a smooth trip," Charles said.

"I didn't mean the trip."

"We're okay, Aunt Lois."

"She says you want to go to Europe with her."

"It didn't take her long," Charles said, "did it. I just suggested it in the car on the way here. It was just an idea."

"Let me take one of those bags, honey. I don't want her to think I came out here just to jabber with you, although that's exactly why I did come out."

Charles handed her his own small suitcase.

"You like my boots?" she said. "I figured I could attract a handsome fireman with them." She modeled them for him, turning.

"They're a little big for you, Aunt Lois."

"You're no fun."

He was struggling with his mother's suitcases.

"I guess you noticed that I moved the chair. You looked a little surprised. But when I got back here after the funeral I walked in there and—well, there it was, right where he always was whenever you all visited. I used to tease him about sleeping in it all day—you remember. We all used to tease him about it. Well, I didn't want you to walk in and see it that way—"

Charles closed the trunk of the car and hefted the suitcases, facing her.

"You want to go home, don't you," she said.

It seemed to him that she had always had a way of reading him. "I want everything to be back the way it was," he said.

"I know," Aunt Lois said.

He followed her back to the house. On the porch she turned and gave him a sad look and then forced a smile. "You're an intelligent young man, and a very good one, too. So serious and sweet—a very dear, sweet boy."

He might have mumbled a thank-you, he didn't really know. He was embarrassed and confused and sick at heart; he had thought he wanted this visit. Aunt Lois kissed him on the cheek, then stood back and sighed. "I'm going to need your help about something. Boy, am I ever."

"What's the matter?" he said.

"It's nothing. It's just a situation." She sighed again. She wasn't looking at him now. "I don't know why, but I find it—well, reassuring, somehow, that we—we—leave such a gaping hole in everything when we go."

He just stood there, weighted down with the bags.

"Well," she said, and opened the door for him.

CHARLES'S mother said she wanted to sit up and talk, but she kept nodding off. Finally she was asleep. When Aunt Lois began gently to wake her, to walk her in to her bed, Charles excused himself and made his way to his own bed. A few moments later he heard Aunt Lois in the kitchen. As had always been her custom, she would drink one last cup of coffee before retiring. He lay awake, hearing the soft tink of her cup against the saucer, and at last he began to drift. But in a little while he was fully awake again. Aunt Lois was moving through the house turning the lights off, and soon she too was down for the night. Charles stared through the shadows of the doorway to what he knew was the entrance to the living room, and listened to the house settle into itself. Outside, there were the hum and whoosh of traffic on the overpass, and the occasional sighing rush of rain at the window, like surf. Yet he knew he wouldn't sleep. He was thinking of summer nights in a cottage on Cape Cod, when his family was happy, and he lay with the sun burning in his skin and listened to the adults talking and laughing out on the screened porch, the sound of the bay rushing like this rain at this window. He couldn't sleep. Turning in the bed, he cupped his hands over his face.

A year ago, two years—at some time and in some way that was beyond him—his parents had grown quiet with each other, a change had started, and he could remember waking up one morning near the end of his last school year with a deep sense that something somewhere would go so wrong, was already so wrong that there would be no coming back from it. There was a change in the chemistry of the household that sapped his will, that took the breath out of him and left him in an exhaustion so profound that even the small energy necessary for speech seemed unavailable to him. This past summer, the first summer out of high school, he had done nothing with himself; he had found nothing he wanted to do, nothing he could feel anything at all about. He looked for a job because his parents insisted that he do so; it was an ordeal of walking, of managing to talk, to fill out applications, and in the end he found nothing. The summer wore on and his father grew angry and sullen with him. Charles was a disappointment and knew it; he was overweight, and seemed lazy, and he couldn't find a way to explain himself. His mother thought there might be something physically wrong, and so then there were doctors, and medical examinations to endure. What he wanted was to stay in the house and have his parents be the people that they once were—happy, fortunate people with interest in each other and warmth and humor between them. And then one day in September his father keeled over on the sidewalk outside a restaurant in New York, and Charles had begun to be this person he now was, someone hurting in this irremediable way, lying awake in his aunt's house in the middle of a cold December night, wishing with all his heart it were some other time, some other place.

IN the morning, after breakfast, Aunt Lois began to talk about how good it would be to have people at her table for dinner on Christmas Eve. She had opened the draperies wide, to watch the snow fall outside. The snow had started before sunrise, but nothing had accumulated yet; it was melting as it hit the ground. Aunt Lois talked about how Christmasy it felt, and about getting a tree to put up, about making a big turkey dinner. "I don't think anybody should be alone on Christmas," she said. "Do you, Marie?"

"Not unless they want to," Marie said.

"Right, and who wants to be alone on Christmas?"

"Lois, I suppose you're going to come to the point soon."

"Well," Aunt Lois said, "I guess I am driving at something. I've invited someone over to dinner on Christmas Eve."

"Who."

"It's someone you know."

"Lois, please."

"I ran into him on jury duty last June," Aunt Lois said. "Can you imagine? After all these years—and we've become very good friends again. I mean I'd court him if I thought I had a chance."

"Lois, who are we talking about?"

"Well," Aunt Lois said, "It's Bill Downs."

Marie stood. "You're not serious."

"It has nothing to do with anything," Lois said. "To tell you the truth, I invited them before I knew you were coming."

"Them?"

"He has a cousin visiting. I told him they could both come."

"Who's Bill Downs?" Charles asked.

"He's nobody," said his mother.

"He's somebody from a long time ago," Aunt Lois said. They had spoken almost in unison. Aunt Lois went on: "His cousin just lost his wife. Well—last year. Bill didn't want him to be alone. He says he's a very interesting man—"

"Lois, I don't care if he's the King of England."

"I didn't mean anything by it," Aunt Lois said. "Don't make it into something it isn't. Look at us, anyway—look how depleted we are. I want people here. I don't want it just the three of us on Christmas. You have Charles; I'm the last one in this family, Marie. And this—this isn't just *your* grief. Lawrence was my brother. I didn't want to be alone—do you want me to spell it out for you?"

Marie now seemed too confused to speak. She only glanced at Charles, then turned and left the room. Her door closed quietly. Aunt Lois sat back against the cushions of the sofa and shut her eyes for a moment.

"Who's Bill Downs?" Charles said.

When she opened her eyes it was as if she had just noticed him there. "The whole thing is just silly. We were all kids together. It was a million years ago."

Charles said nothing. In the fireplace a single charred log hissed. Aunt Lois sat forward and took a cigarette from her pack and lighted it. "I wonder what you're thinking."

"I don't know."

"Do you have a steady girl, Charles?"

He nodded. The truth was that he was too shy, too aware of his girth and the floridness of his complexion, too nervous and clumsy to be more than the clownish, kindly friend he was to the girls he knew.

"Do you think you'll go on and marry her?"

"Who?" he said.

"Your girl."

"Oh," he said, "probably not."

"Some people do, of course. And some don't. Some people go on and meet other people. Do you see? When I met your mother, your father was away at college."

"I think I had this figured out already, Aunt Lois."

"Well—then that's who Bill Downs is." She got to her feet, with some effort, then stood gazing down at him. "This just isn't the way it looks, though. And everybody will just have to believe me about it."

"I believe you," Charles said.

"She doesn't," said Aunt Lois, "and now she's probably going to start lobbying to go home."

Charles shook his head.

"I hope you won't let her talk you into it."

"Nobody's going anywhere," Marie said, coming into the room. She sat down on the sofa and opened the morning paper, and when she spoke now it was as if she were not even attentive to her own words. "Though it would serve you right if everybody deserted you out of embarrassment."

"You might think about *me* a little, Marie. You might think how *I* feel in all this."

Marie put the newspaper down on her lap and looked at her. "I am thinking of you. If I wasn't thinking of you I'd be in the car this minute, heading north, whether Charles would come or not."

"Well, fine," Aunt Lois said, and stormed out of the room.

• • •

A little later, Charles and Marie went into the city. They parked the car in a garage on H Street and walked over to Lafayette Square. It was still snowing, but the ground was too warm; it wouldn't stick. Charles said, "Might as well be raining," and realized that neither of them had spoken since they had pulled away from Aunt Lois's house.

"Charles," his mother said, and then seemed to stop herself. "Never mind."

"What?" he said.

"Nothing. It's easy to forget that you're only eighteen. I forget sometimes, that's all."

Charles sensed that this wasn't what she had started to say, but kept silent. They crossed the square and entered a sandwich shop on Seventeenth Street, to warm themselves with a cup of coffee. They sat at a table by the window and looked out at the street, the people walking by—shoppers mostly, burdened with packages.

"Where's the Lafayette Hotel from here?" Charles asked.

"Oh, honey, they tore that down a long time ago."

"Where was it?"

"You can't see it from here." She took a handkerchief out of her purse and touched the corners of her eyes with it. "The cold makes my eyes sting. How about you?"

"It's the wind," Charles said.

She looked at him. "My ministering angel."

"Mom," he said.

Now she looked out the window. "Your father would be proud of you now." She bowed her head slightly, fumbling with her purse, and then she was crying. She held the handkerchief to her nose, and the tears dropped down over her hand.

"Mom," he said, reaching for her wrist.

She withdrew from him a little. "No, you don't understand."

"Let's go," Charles said.

"I don't think I could stand to be home now, Charles. Not on Christmas. Not this Christmas."

Charles paid the check and then went back to the table to help her into her coat. "Goddamn Lois," she said, pulling the furry collar up to cover her ears.

"TELL me about your girlfriend," Aunt Lois said.

He shrugged this off.

They were sitting in the kitchen, breaking up bread for the dressing, while Marie napped on the sofa in the living room. Aunt Lois had brought the turkey out and set it on the counter. The meat deep in its breast still had to thaw, she told Charles. She was talking just to talk. Things had been very cool since the morning, and Charles was someone to talk to.

"Won't even tell me her name?"

"I'm not really going with anybody," he said.

"A handsome boy like you."

"Aunt Lois, could we talk about something else?"

She said, "All right. Tell me what you did all fall."

"I took care of the house."

"Did you read any good books or see any movies or take anybody out besides your mother?"

"Sure," he said.

"Okay, tell me about it."

"What do you want to know?"

"I want to know what you did all fall."

"What is this?" Charles said.

She spoke quickly. "I apologize for prying. I won't say another word."

"Look," he said, "Aunt Lois, I'm not keeping myself from anything right now. I couldn't have concentrated in school in September."

"I know," she said, "I know."

There was a long silence.

"I wonder if it's too late for me to get married and have a bunch of babies," she said suddenly. "I think I'd like the noise they'd make."

THAT night, they watched Christmas specials. Charles dozed in the lounge chair by the fireplace, a magazine on his lap, and the women sat on the sofa. No one spoke. On television, celebrities sang old Christmas songs, and during the commercials other celebrities appealed to the various yearnings for cheer and happiness and possessions, and the thrill of giving. In a two-hour cartoon with music and production numbers, Scrooge made his night-long journey to wisdom and love; the Cratchits were portrayed as church mice. Aunt Lois remarked that this was cute, and no one answered her. Charles feigned sleep. When the news came on, Aunt Lois turned the television off, and they said good night. Charles kissed them both on the cheek, and went to his room. For a long while after he lay down, he heard them talking low. They had gone to Aunt Lois's room. He couldn't distinguish words, but the tones were chilly and serious. He rolled over on his side and punched the pillow into shape and stared at the faint outline of trees outside the window, trying not to hear. The voices continued, and he heard his mother's voice rising, so that he could almost make out words now. His mother said something about last summer, and then both women were silent. A few moments later, Aunt Lois came marching down the hall past his door, on into the kitchen, where she opened cabinets and slammed them, and ran water. She was going to make coffee, she said, when Marie called to her. If she wanted a cup of coffee in her own house at any hour of the night she'd have coffee.

Charles waited a minute or so, then got up, put his robe on, and went in to her. She sat at the table, arms folded, waiting for the water to boil.

"It's sixty dollars for a good Christmas tree," she said. "A ridiculous amount of money."

Charles sat down across from her.

"You're just like your father," she said, "you placate. And I think he placated your mother too much—that's what I think."

He said, "Come on, Aunt Lois."

"Well, she makes me so mad, I can't help it. She doesn't want to go home and she doesn't want to stay here and she won't listen to the slightest suggestion about you or the way you've been nursemaiding her for four months. And she's just going to stay mad at me all week. Now, you tell me."

"I just wish everybody would calm down," Charles said.

She stood and turned her back to him and set about making her coffee.

ACCORDING to the medical report, Charles's father had suffered a massive coronary occlusion, and death was almost instantaneous; it could not have been attended with much pain. Perhaps there had been a second's recognition, but little more than that. The doctor wanted Charles and his mother to know that the speed with which an attack like that kills is a blessing. In his sleep, Charles heard the doctor's voice saying this, and then he was watching his father fall down on the sidewalk outside the restaurant; people walked by and stared, and Charles looked at their faces, the faces of strangers.

He woke trembling in the dark, the only one awake on Christmas Eve morning. He lay on his side, facing the window, and watched the dawn arrive, and at last someone was up, moving around in the kitchen.

It was his mother. She was making coffee. "You're up early," she said.

"I dreamed about Dad."

"I dream about him too," she said. She opened the refrigerator. "Good God, there's a leg of lamb in here. Where did this come from? What in the world is that woman thinking of? The turkey's big enough for eight people."

"Maybe it's for tomorrow."

"And don't always defend her, either, Charles. She's not infallible, you know."

"I never said she was."

"None of them—your father wasn't. I mean—" she closed the refrigerator and took a breath. "He wouldn't want you to put him on a pedestal."

"I didn't," Charles said.

"People are people," she said. "They don't always add up."

This didn't seem to require a response.

"And I've known Lois since she was seventeen years old. I know how she thinks."

"I'm not defending anybody," he said, "I'm just the one in between everything here. I wish you'd both just leave me out of it."

"Go get dressed," she said. "Nobody's putting you in between anybody."

"Mom."

"No—you're right. I won't involve you. Now really, go get dressed." She looked as though she might begin to cry again. She patted him on the wrist and then went back to the refrigerator. "I wanted something in here," she said, opening it. There were dark blue veins forking over her ankles. She looked old and thin and afraid and lonely, and he turned his eyes away.

THE three of them went to shop for a tree. Charles drove. They looked in three places and couldn't agree on anything, and when it began to rain Aunt Lois took matters into her own hands. She made them wait in the car while she picked out the tree she wanted for what was, after all, her living room. They got the tree home, and had to saw off part of the trunk to get it up, but when it was finished, ornamented and wound with popcorn and tinsel, they all agreed that it was a handsome tree —a round, long-needled pine that looked like a jolly rotund elf, with its sawed-off trunk and its top listing slightly to the left under the weight of a tinfoil star. They turned its lights on and stood admiring it, and for a while there was something of the warmth of other Christmases in the air. Work on the decorations, and all the cooperation required to get everything accomplished seemed to have created a kind of peace between the two women. They spent the early part of the evening wrapping presents for the morning, each in his own room with his gifts for the others, and then Aunt Lois put the television on, and went about her business, getting the dinner ready. She wanted no help from anyone, she said, but Marie began to help anyway, and Aunt Lois did nothing to stop her. Charles sat in the lounge chair and watched a parade. It was the halftime of a football game, but he was not interested in it, and soon he had begun to doze again. He sank deep, and there were no dreams, and then Aunt Lois was telling him to wake up. "Charles," she said, "they're here." He sat forward in the chair, a little startled, and Aunt Lois laughed. "Wake up, son," she said. Charles saw a man standing by the Christmas tree, smiling at him. Another man sat on the sofa, his legs spread a little to make room for his stomach; he looked blown up, his neck bulging over the collar of his shirt.

"Charles," Aunt Lois said, indicating the man on the sofa, "this is Mr. Rainy."

Mr. Rainy was smiling in an almost imbecilic way, not really looking at anyone.

"This is Charles," Aunt Lois said to him.

They shook hands. "Nice to meet you," Mr. Rainy said. He had a soft, high-pitched voice.

"And this is Mr. Downs."

Charles looked at him, took the handshake he offered. Bill Downs was tall and a little stooped, and he seemed very uneasy. He looked around the room, and his hands went into his pockets and then flew up to his hair, which was wild-looking and very sparse.

"Marie will be out any time, I'm sure," Aunt Lois said in a voice that, to Charles at least, sounded anything but sure. "In the meantime, can I get anybody a drink?"

No one wanted anything right away. Mr. Rainy had brought two bottles of champagne, which Aunt Lois took from him and put on ice in the kitchen. The two men sat on the sofa across from Charles, and the football game provided them with something to look at. Charles caught himself watching Bill Downs, and thinking about how his mother had once felt something for him. It was hard to picture them together, as it was hard not to stare at the man, at his skinny hands, never still in the long-legged lap, and the nervous way he looked around the room. He did not look past forty years old, except for the thinning hair.

"You boys get your football watching before dinner," Aunt Lois said, coming back into the room. "I won't have it after we begin to eat."

"I'm not much of a football fan," Bill Downs said.

Charles almost blurted out that his father had loved football. He kept silent. In the next moment, Marie made her entrance. It struck Charles exactly that way: that it was an entrance, thoroughly dramatic and calculated to have an effect. It was vivacious in a nervous, almost automatic way. She crossed the room to kiss him on the forehead and then she turned to face the two men on the sofa. "Bill, you haven't changed a bit."

Downs was clambering over himself to get to his feet. "You either, Marie."

"Merry Christmas," Mr. Rainy said, also trying to rise.

"Oh, don't get up," Marie was saying.

Charles sat in his chair and watched them make their way through the introductions and the polite talk before dinner. He watched his mother, mostly. He knew exactly what she was feeling, understood the embarrassment and the nervousness out of which every gesture and word came, and yet something in him hated her for it, felt betrayed by it. When she went with the two men into the kitchen to open one of the bottles of champagne, he got out of the chair and faced Aunt Lois, whose expression seemed to be saying "Well?" as if this were only what one should have expected. He shook his head, and she said, "Come on."

They went into the kitchen. Marie was leaning against the counter with a glass of champagne in her hand. Charles decided that he couldn't look at her. She and Bill Downs were talking about the delicious smell of the turkey.

"I didn't have Thanksgiving dinner this year," Mr. Rainy was saying. "You know, I lost my wife. I just didn't feel like anything, you know."

"This is a hard time of year," Aunt Lois said.

"I simply don't know how to act anymore," Mr. Rainy said.

Charles backed quietly away from them. He took himself to the living room and the television, where everyone seemed to know everyone else. They were all celebrating Christmas on television, and then the football game was on again. Charles got into his coat and stepped out onto the porch, intending at first just to take a few deep breaths, to shake if he could this feeling of betrayal and anger that had risen in him. It was already dark. The rain had turned to mist again. When the wind blew, cold drops splattered on the eaves of the porch. The cars and trucks racing by on the overpass at the end of the block seemed to traverse a part of the sky. Charles moved to the steps of the porch, and behind him the door opened. He turned to see his mother, who came out after glancing into the house, apparently wanting to be sure they would be alone. She wasn't wearing her coat, and he started to say something about the chill she would get when the expression on her face stopped him.

"What do you expect from me, Charles?"

He couldn't speak for a moment.

She advanced across the porch, already shivering. "What am I supposed to do?"

"I don't know what you're talking about."

"Oh, God." She paced back and forth in front of him, her arms wrapped around herself. Somewhere off in the misty dark, a group of people were singing carols. The voices came in on a gust of wind, and when the wind died they were gone. "God," she said again. Then she muttered, "Christmas."

"I wish it was two years ago," Charles said suddenly.

She had stopped pacing. "It won't ever be two years ago, and you'd better get used to that right now."

Charles was silent.

"You're turning what you remember into a paradise," she said, "and I've helped you get a good start on it."

"I'm not," Charles said, "I'm not doing that at all. I remember the way it was last summer when I wasn't—when I couldn't do anything and he couldn't make me do anything, and you and he were so different with each other—" He halted. He wasn't looking at her.

"Go on," she said.

He said, "Nothing."

"What went on between your father and I is nobody's business."

"I didn't say it was."

"It had nothing to do with you, Charles."

"All right," he said.

She was shivering so hard now that her voice quavered when she spoke. "I wish I could *make* it all right, but I can't."

Charles reached for her, put his arms around her, and she cried into the hollow of his shoulder. They stood that way for a while, and the wind blew and again there was the sound of the carolers.

"Mom," Charles said, "he was going to leave us, wasn't he."

She removed herself, produced a handkerchief from somewhere in her skirt, and touched it to her nose, still trembling, staring down. Then she breathed out as if something had given way inside her, and Charles could see that she was gathering herself, trying not to show whatever it was that had just gone through her. When she raised her eyes she gave him the softest, the kindest look. "Not you," she said. Then: "Don't think such things." She turned from him, stepped up into the doorway, and the light there made a willowy shadow of her. "Don't stay out here too long, son. Don't be rude."

When she had closed the door, he walked down the street to the overpass and stood below it, his hands deep in his coat pockets. It wasn't extremely cold out yet, but he was cold. He was cold, and he shook, and above him the traffic whooshed by. He turned and faced the house, beginning to cry now, and a sound came out of him that he put his hands to his mouth to stop. When a car came along the road he ducked back into the deeper shadow of the overpass, but he had been seen. The car pulled toward him, and a policeman shined a light on him.

"What're you doing there, fella?"

"Nothing," Charles said. "My father died."

The policeman kept the light on him for a few seconds, then turned it off. He said, "Go on home, son," and drove away.

Charles watched until the taillights disappeared in the mist. It was quiet; even the traffic on the overpass had ceased for a moment. The police car came back, slowing as it passed him, then going on, and once more it was quiet. He turned and looked at the house with its Christmas tree shimmering in the window, and in that instant it seemed to contain only the light and tangle of adulthood; it was their world, so far from him. He wiped his eyes with the backs of his hands, beginning to cry again. No, it wasn't so far. It wasn't so far at all. Up the street, Aunt Lois opened her door and called his name. But she couldn't see him, and he didn't answer her.

WHAT FEELS LIKE THE WORLD

V ERY EARLY IN THE MORNING, too early, he hears her trying to jump rope out on the sidewalk below his bedroom window. He wakes to the sound of her shoes on the concrete, her breathless counting as she jumps—never more than three times in succession—and fails again to find the right rhythm, the proper spring in her legs to achieve the thing, to be a girl jumping rope. He gets up and moves to the window and, parting the curtain only slightly, peers out at her. For some reason he feels he must be stealthy, must not let her see him gazing at her from this window. He thinks of the heartless way children tease the imperfect among them, and then he closes the curtain.

She is his only granddaughter, the unfortunate inheritor of his big-boned genes, his tendency toward bulk, and she is on a self-induced program of exercise and dieting, to lose weight. This is in preparation for the last meeting of the PTA, during which children from the fifth and sixth grades will put on a gymnastics demonstration. There will be a vaulting horse and a mini-trampoline, and everyone is to participate. She wants to be able to do at least as well as the other children in her class, and so she has been trying exercises to improve her coordination and lose the weight that keeps her rooted to the ground. For the past two weeks she has been eating only one meal a day, usually lunch, since that's the meal she eats at school, and swallowing cans of juice at other mealtimes. He's afraid of anorexia but trusts her calm determination to get ready for the event. There seems no desperation, none of the classic symptoms of the disease. Indeed, this project she's set for herself seems quite sane: to lose ten pounds, and to be able to get over the vaulting horse—in fact, she hopes that she'll be able to do a handstand on it and, curling her head and shoulders, flip over to stand upright on the other side. This, she has told him, is the outside hope. And in two weeks of very grown-up discipline and single-minded effort, that hope has mostly disappeared; she's still the only child in the fifth grade who has not even been able to propel herself over the horse, and this is the day of the event. She will have one last chance to practice at school today, and so she's up this early, out on the lawn, straining, pushing herself.

He dresses quickly and heads downstairs. The ritual in the mornings is simplified by the fact that neither of them is eating breakfast. He makes the orange juice, puts vitamins on a saucer for them both. When he glances out the living-room window, he sees that she is now doing somersaults in the dewy grass. She does three of them while he watches, and he isn't stealthy this time but stands in the window with what he hopes is an approving, unworried look on his face. After each somersault she pulls her sweat shirt down, takes a deep breath, and begins again, the arms coming down slowly, the head ducking slowly under; it's as if she falls on her back, sits up, and then stands up. Her cheeks are ruddy with effort. The moistness of the grass is on the sweat suit, and in the ends of her hair. It will rain this morning—there's thunder beyond the trees at the end of the street. He taps on the window, gestures, smiling, for her to come in. She waves at him, indicates that she wants him to watch her, so he watches her. He applauds when she's finished—three hard, slow tumbles. She claps her hands together as if to remove dust from them and comes trotting to the door. As she moves by him, he tells her she's asking for a bad cold, letting herself get wet so early in the morning. It's his place to nag. Her glance at him acknowledges this.

"I can't get the rest of me to follow my head," she says about the somersaults.

They go into the kitchen, and she sits down, pops a vitamin into her mouth, and takes a swallow of the orange juice. "I guess I'm not going to make it over that vaulting horse after all," she says suddenly.

"Sure you will."

"I don't care." She seems to pout. This is the first sign of true discouragement she's shown.

He's been waiting for it. "Brenda—honey, sometimes people aren't good at these things. I mean, I was never any good at it."

"I bet you were," she says. "I bet you're just saying that to make me feel better."

"No," he says, "really."

He's been keeping to the diet with her, though there have been times during the day when he's cheated. He no longer has a job, and the days are long; he's hungry all the time. He pretends to her that he's still going on to work in the mornings after he walks her to school, because he wants to keep her sense of the daily balance of things, of a predictable and orderly routine, intact. He believes this is the best way to deal with grief —simply to go on with things, to keep them as much as possible as they have always been. Being out of work doesn't worry him, really: he has enough money in savings to last awhile. At sixty-one, he's almost eligible for Social Security, and he gets monthly checks from the girl's father, who lives with another woman, and other children, in Oregon. The father has been very good about keeping up the payments, though he never visits or calls. Probably he thinks the money buys him the privilege of remaining aloof, now that Brenda's mother is gone. Brenda's mother used to say he was the type of man who learned early that there was nothing of substance anywhere in his soul, and spent the rest of his life trying to hide this fact from himself. No one was more upright, she would say, no one more honorable, and God help you if you ever had to live with him. Brenda's father was the subject of bitter sarcasm and scorn. And yet, perhaps not so surprisingly, Brenda's mother would call him in those months just after the divorce, when Brenda was still only a toddler, and she would try to get the baby to say things to him over the phone. And she would sit there with Brenda on her lap and cry after she had hung up.

"I had a doughnut yesterday at school," Brenda says now.

"That's lunch. You're supposed to eat lunch."

"I had spaghetti, too. And three pieces of garlic bread. And pie. And a big salad."

"What's one doughnut?"

"Well, and I didn't eat anything the rest of the day."

"I know," her grandfather says. "See?"

They sit quiet for a little while. Sometimes they're shy with each other—more so lately. They're used to the absence of her mother by now—it's been almost a year—but they still find themselves missing a beat now and then, like a heart with a valve almost closed. She swallows the last of her juice and then gets up and moves to the living room, to stand gazing out at the yard. Big drops have begun to fall. It's a storm, with rising wind and, now, very loud thunder. Lightning branches across the sky, and the trees in the yard disappear in sheets of rain. He has come to her side, and he pretends an interest in the details of the weather, remarking on the heaviness of the rain, the strength of the wind. "Some storm," he says finally. "I'm glad we're not out in it." He wishes he could tell what she's thinking, where the pain is; he wishes he could be certain of the harmlessness of his every word. "Honey," he ventures, "we could play hooky today. If you want to."

"Don't you think I can do it?" she says.

"I know you can."

She stares at him a moment and then looks away, out at the storm.

"It's terrible out there, isn't it?" he says. "Look at that lightning."

"You don't think I can do it," she says.

"No. I know you can. Really."

"Well, I probably can't."

"Even if you can't. Lots of people—lots of people never do anything like that."

"I'm the only one who can't that *I* know."

"Well, there's lots of people. The whole thing is silly, Brenda. A year from now it won't mean anything at all—you'll see."

She says nothing.

"Is there some pressure at school to do it?"

"No." Her tone is simple, matter-of-fact, and she looks directly at him.

"You're sure."

She's sure. And of course, he realizes, there *is* pressure; there's the pressure of being one among other children, and being the only one among them who can't do a thing.

"Honey," he says lamely, "it's not that important."

When she looks at him this time, he sees something scarily unchildlike in her expression, some perplexity that she seems to pull down into herself. "It is too important," she says.

HE drives her to school. The rain is still being blown along the street and above the low roofs of the houses. By the time they arrive, no more than five minutes from the house, it has begun to let up.

"If it's completely stopped after school," she says, "can we walk home?"

"Of course," he says. "Why wouldn't we?"

She gives him a quick wet kiss on the cheek. "Bye, Pops."

He knows she doesn't like it when he waits for her to get inside, and still he hesitates. There's always the apprehension that he'll look away or drive off just as she thinks of something she needs from him, or that she'll wave to him and he won't see her. So he sits here with the car engine idling, and she walks quickly up the sidewalk and into the building. In the few seconds before the door swings shut, she turns and gives him a wave, and he waves back. The door is closed now. Slowly he lets the car glide forward, still watching the door. Then he's down the driveway, and he heads back to the house.

IT'S hard to decide what to do with his time. Mostly he stays in the house, watches television, reads the newspapers. There are household tasks, but he can't do anything she might notice, since he's supposed to be at work during these hours. Sometimes, just to please himself, he drives over to the bank and visits with his old co-workers, though there doesn't seem to be much to talk about anymore and he senses that he makes them all uneasy. Today he lies down on the sofa in the living room and rests awhile. At the windows the sun begins to show, and he thinks of driving into town, perhaps stopping somewhere to eat a light breakfast. He accuses himself with the thought and then gets up and turns on the television. There isn't anything of interest to watch, but he watches anyway. The sun is bright now out on the lawn, and the wind is the same, gusting and shaking the window frames. On television he sees feasts of incredible sumptuousness, almost nauseating in the impossible brightness and succulence of the food: advertisements from cheese companies, dairy associations, the makers of cookies and pizza, the sellers of seafood and steaks. He's angry with himself for wanting to cheat on the diet. He thinks of Brenda at school, thinks of crowds of children, and it comes to him more painfully than ever that he can't protect her. Not any more than he could ever protect her mother.

He goes outside and walks up the drying sidewalk to the end of the block. The sun has already dried most of the morning's rain, and the wind is warm. In the sky are great stormy Matterhorns of cumulus and wide patches of the deepest blue. It's a beautiful day, and he decides to walk over to the school. Nothing in him voices this decision; he simply begins to walk. He knows without having to think about it that he can't allow her to see him, yet he feels compelled to take the risk that she might; he feels a helpless wish to watch over her, and, beyond this, he entertains the vague notion that by seeing her in her world he might be better able to be what she needs in his.

So he walks the four blocks to the school and stands just beyond the playground, in a group of shading maples that whisper and sigh in the wind. The playground is empty. A bell rings somewhere in the building, but no one comes out. It's not even eleven o'clock in the morning. He's too late for morning recess and too early for the afternoon one. He feels as though she watches him make his way back down the street.

HIS neighbor, Mrs. Eberhard, comes over for lunch. It's a thing they planned, and he's forgotten about it. She knocks on the door, and when he opens it she smiles and says, "I knew you'd forget." She's on a diet too, and is carrying what they'll eat: two apples, some celery and carrots. It's all in a clear plastic bag, and she holds it toward him in the palms of her hands as though it were piping hot from an oven. Jane Eberhard is relatively new in the neighborhood. When Brenda's mother died, Jane offered to cook meals and regulate things, and for a while she was like another member of the family. She's moved into their lives now, and sometimes they all forget the circumstances under which the friendship began. She's a solid, large-hipped woman of fifty-eight, with clear, young blue eyes and gray hair. The thing she's good at is sympathy; there's something oddly unspecific about it, as if it were a beam she simply radiates.

"You look so worried," she says now, "I think you should be proud of her."

They're sitting in the living room, with the plastic bag on the coffee table before them. She's eating a stick of celery.

"I've never seen a child that age put such demands on herself," she says.

"I don't know what it's going to do to her if she doesn't make it over the damn thing," he says.

"It'll disappoint her. But she'll get over it."

"I don't guess you can make it tonight."

"Can't," she says. "Really. I promised my mother I'd take her to the ocean this weekend. I have to go pick her up tonight."

"I walked over to the school a little while ago."

"Are you sure you're not putting more into this than she is?"

"She was up at dawn this morning, Jane. Didn't you see her?"

Mrs. Eberhard nods. "I saw her."

"Well?" he says.

She pats his wrist. "I'm sure it won't matter a month from now."

"No," he says, "that's not true. I mean, I wish I could believe you. But I've never seen a kid work so hard."

"Maybe she'll make it."

"Yes," he says. "Maybe."

Mrs. Eberhard sits considering for a moment, tapping the stick of celery against her lower lip. "You think it's tied to the accident in some way, don't you?"

"I don't know," he says, standing, moving across the room. "I can't get through somehow. It's been all this time and I still don't know. She keeps it all to herself—all of it. All I can do is try to be there when she wants me to be there. I don't know —I don't even know what to say to her."

"You're doing all you can do, then."

"Her mother and I . . ." he begins. "She—we never got along that well."

"You can't worry about that now."

Mrs. Eberhard's advice is always the kind of practical good advice that's impossible to follow.

He comes back to the sofa and tries to eat one of the apples, but his appetite is gone. This seems ironic to him. "I'm not hungry now," he says.

"Sometimes worry is the best thing for a diet."

"I've always worried. It never did me any good, but I worried."

"I'll tell you," Mrs. Eberhard says. "It's a terrific misfortune to have to be raised by a human being."

He doesn't feel like listening to this sort of thing, so he asks her about her husband, who is with the government in some capacity that requires him to be both secretive and mobile. He's always off to one country or another, and this week he's in India. It's strange to think of someone traveling as much as he does without getting hurt or killed. Mrs. Eberhard says she's so used to his being gone all the time that next year, when he retires, it'll take a while to get used to having him underfoot. In fact, he's not a very likable man; there's something murky and unpleasant about him. The one time Mrs. Eberhard brought him to visit, he sat in the living room and seemed to regard everyone with detached curiosity, as if they were all specimens on a dish under a lens. Brenda's grandfather had invited some old friends over from the bank—everyone was being careful not to let on that he wasn't still going there every day. It was an awkward two hours, and Mrs. Eberhard's husband sat with his hands folded over his rounded belly, his eyebrows arched. When he spoke, his voice was cultivated and quiet, full of self-satisfaction and haughtiness. They had been speaking in low tones about how Jane Eberhard had moved in to take over after the accident, and Mrs. Eberhard's husband cleared his throat, held his fist gingerly to his mouth, pursed his lips, and began a soft-spoken, lecture-like monologue about his belief that there's no such thing as an accident. His considered opinion was that there are subconscious explanations for everything. Apparently, he thought he was entertaining everyone. He sat with one leg crossed over the other and held forth in his calm, magisterial voice, explaining how everything can be reduced to a matter of conscious or subconscious will. Finally his wife asked him to let it alone, please, drop the subject.

"For example," he went on, "there are many collisions on the highway in which no one appears to have applied brakes before impact, as if something in the victims had decided on death. And of course there are the well-known cases of people stopped on railroad tracks, with plenty of time to get off, who simply do not move. Perhaps it isn't being frozen by the perception of one's fate but a matter of decision making, of will. The victim decides on his fate."

"I think we've had enough, now," Jane Eberhard said.

The inappropriateness of what he had said seemed to dawn on him then. He shifted in his seat and grew very quiet, and when the evening was over he took Brenda's grandfather by the elbow and apologized. But even in the apology there seemed to be a species of condescension, as if he were really only sorry for the harsh truth of what he had wrongly deemed it necessary to say. When everyone was gone, Brenda said, "I don't like that man."

"Is it because of what he said about accidents?" her grandfather asked.

She shook her head. "I just don't like him."

"It's not true, what he said, honey. An accident is an accident."

She said, "I know." But she would not return his gaze.

"Your mother wasn't very happy here, but she didn't want to leave us. Not even—you know, without . . . without knowing it or anything."

"He wears perfume," she said, still not looking at him.

"It's cologne. Yes, he does—too much of it."

"It smells," she said.

In the afternoon he walks over to the school. The sidewalks are crowded with children, and they all seem to recognize him. They carry their books and papers and their hair is windblown and they run and wrestle with each other in the yards. The sun's high and very hot, and most of the clouds have broken apart and scattered. There's still a fairly steady wind, but it's gentler now, and there's no coolness in it.

Brenda is standing at the first crossing street down the hill from the school. She's surrounded by other children yet seems separate from them somehow. She sees him and smiles. He waits on his side of the intersection for her to cross, and when she reaches him he's careful not to show any obvious affection, knowing it embarrasses her.

"How was your day?" he begins.

"Mr. Clayton tried to make me quit today."

He waits.

"I didn't get over," she says. "I didn't even get close."

"What did Mr. Clayton say?"

"Oh—you know. That it's not important. That kind of stuff."

"Well," he says gently, "*is* it so important?"

"I don't know." She kicks at something in the grass along the edge of the sidewalk—a piece of a pencil someone else had discarded. She bends, picks it up, examines it, and then drops it. This is exactly the kind of slow, daydreaming behavior that used to make him angry and impatient with her mother. They walk on. She's concentrating on the sidewalk before them, and they walk almost in step.

"I'm sure I could never do a thing like going over a vaulting horse when I was in school," he says.

"Did they have that when you were in school?"

He smiles. "It was hard getting everything into the caves. But sure, we had that sort of thing. We were an advanced tribe. We had fire, too."

"Okay," she's saying, "okay, okay."

"Actually, with me, it was pull-ups. We all had to do pull-ups. And I just couldn't do them. I don't think I ever accomplished a single one in my life."

"I can't do pull-ups," she says.

"They're hard to do."

"Everybody in the fifth and sixth grades can get over the vaulting horse," she says.

How much she reminds him of her mother. There's a certain mobility in her face, a certain willingness to assert herself in the smallest gesture of the eyes and mouth. She has her mother's green eyes, and now he tells her this. He's decided to try this. He's standing, quite shy, in her doorway, feeling like an intruder. She's sitting on the floor, one leg outstretched, the other bent at the knee. She tries to touch her forehead to the knee of the outstretched leg, straining, and he looks away.

"You know?" he says. "They're just the same color—just that shade of green."

"What was my grandmother like?" she asks, still straining.

"She was a lot like your mother."

"I'm never going to get married."

"Of course you will. Well, I mean—if you want to, you will."

"How come you didn't ever get married again?"

"Oh," he says, "I had a daughter to raise, you know."

She changes position, tries to touch her forehead to the other knee.

"I'll tell you, that mother of yours was enough to keep me busy. I mean, I called her double trouble, you know, because I always said she was double the trouble a son would have been. That was a regular joke around here."

"Mom was skinny and pretty."

He says nothing.

"Am I double trouble?"

"No," he says.

"Is that really why you never got married again?"

"Well, no one would have me, either."

"Mom said you liked it."

"Liked what?"

"Being a widow."

"Yes, well," he says.

"Did you?"

"All these questions," he says.

"Do you think about Grandmom a lot?"

"Yes," he says. "That's—you know, we remember our loved ones."

She stands and tries to touch her toes without bending her legs. "Sometimes I dream that Mom's yelling at you and you're yelling back."

"Oh, well," he says, hearing himself say it, feeling himself back down from something. "That's—that's just a dream. You know, it's nothing to think about at all. People who love each other don't agree sometimes—it's—it's nothing. And I'll bet these exercises are going to do the trick."

"I'm very smart, aren't I?"

He feels sick, very deep down. "You're the smartest little girl I ever saw."

"You don't have to come tonight if you don't want to," she says. "You can drop me off if you want, and come get me when it's over."

"Why would I do that?"

She mutters. "*I* would."

"Then why don't we skip it?"

"Lot of good *that* would do," she says.

• • •

FOR dinner they drink apple juice, and he gets her to eat two slices of dry toast. The apple juice is for energy. She drinks it slowly and then goes into her room to lie down, to conserve her strength. She uses the word *conserve*, and he tells her he's so proud of her vocabulary. She thanks him. While she rests, he does a few household chores, trying really just to keep busy. The week's newspapers have been piling up on the coffee table in the living room, the carpets need to be vacuumed, and the whole house needs dusting. None of it takes long enough; none of it quite distracts him. For a while he sits in the living room with a newspaper in his lap and pretends to be reading it. She's restless too. She comes back through to the kitchen, drinks another glass of apple juice, and then joins him in the living room, turns the television on. The news is full of traffic deaths, and she turns to one of the local stations that shows reruns of old situation comedies. They both watch *M*A*S*H* without really taking it in. She bites the cuticles of her nails, and her gaze wanders around the room. It comes to him that he could speak to her now, could make his way through to her grief— and yet he knows that he will do no such thing; he can't even bring himself to speak at all. There are regions of his own sorrow that he simply lacks the strength to explore, and so he sits there watching her restlessness, and at last it's time to go over to the school. Jane Eberhard makes a surprise visit, bearing a handsome good-luck card she's fashioned herself. She kisses Brenda, behaves exactly as if Brenda were going off to some dangerous, faraway place. She stands in the street and waves at them as they pull away, and Brenda leans out the window to shout goodbye. A moment later, sitting back and staring out at the dusky light, she says she feels a surge of energy, and he tells her she's way ahead of all the others in her class, knowing words like *conserve* and *surge*.

"I've always known them," she says.

It's beginning to rain again. Clouds have been rolling in from the east, and the wind shakes the trees. Lightning flickers on the other side of the clouds. Everything seems threatening, relentless. He slows down. There are many cars parked along both sides of the street. "Quite a turnout," he manages.

"Don't worry," she tells him brightly. "I still feel my surge of energy."

It begins to rain as they get out of the car, and he holds his sport coat like a cape to shield her from it. By the time they get to the open front doors, it's raining very hard. People are crowding into the cafeteria, which has been transformed into an arena for the event—chairs set up on four sides of the room as though for a wrestling match. In the center, at the end of the long, bright-red mat, are the vaulting horse and the mini-trampoline. The physical-education teacher, Mr. Clayton, stands at the entrance. He's tall, thin, scraggly-looking, a boy really, no older than twenty-five.

"There's Mr. Clayton," Brenda says.

"I see him."

"Hello, Mr. Clayton."

Mr. Clayton is quite distracted, and he nods quickly, leans toward Brenda, and points to a doorway across the hall. "Go on ahead," he says. Then he nods at her grandfather.

"This is it," Brenda says.

Her grandfather squeezes her shoulder, means to find the best thing to tell her, but in the next confusing minute he's lost her; she's gone among the others and he's being swept along with the crowd entering the cafeteria. He makes his way along the walls behind the chairs, where a few other people have already gathered and are standing. At the other end of the room a man is speaking from a lectern about old business, new officers for the fall. Brenda's grandfather recognizes some of the people in the crowd. A woman looks at him and nods, a familiar face he can't quite place. She turns to look at the speaker. She's holding a baby, and the baby's staring at him over her shoulder. A moment later, she steps back to stand beside him, hefting the baby higher and patting its bottom.

"What a crowd," she says.

He nods.

"It's not usually this crowded."

Again, he nods.

The baby protests, and he touches the miniature fingers of one hand—just a baby, he thinks, and everything still to go through.

"How is—um . . . Brenda?" she says.

"Oh," he says, "fine." And he remembers that she was Brenda's kindergarden teacher. She's heavier than she was then, and her hair is darker. She has a baby now.

"I don't remember all my students," she says, shifting the baby to the other shoulder. "I've been home now for eighteen months, and I'll tell you, it's being at the PTA meeting that makes me see how much I *don't* miss teaching."

He smiles at her and nods again. He's beginning to feel awkward. The man is still speaking from the lectern, a meeting is going on, and this woman's voice is carrying beyond them, though she says everything out of the side of her mouth.

"I remember the way you used to walk Brenda to school every morning. Do you still walk her to school?"

"Yes."

"That's so nice."

He pretends an interest in what the speaker is saying.

"I always thought it was so nice to see how you two got along together—I mean these days it's really rare for the kids even to know who their grandparents *are,* much less have one to walk them to school in the morning. I always thought it was really something." She seems to watch the lectern for a moment, and then speaks to him again, this time in a near whisper. "I hope you won't take this the wrong way or anything, but I just wanted to say how sorry I was about your daughter. I saw it in the paper when Brenda's mother. . . . Well. You know, I just wanted to tell you how sorry. When I saw it in the paper, I thought of Brenda, and how you used to walk her to school. I

lost my sister in an automobile accident, so I know how you feel
—it's a terrible thing. Terrible. An awful thing to have happen.
I mean it's much too sudden and final and everything. I'm
afraid now every time I get into a car." She pauses, pats the
baby's back, then takes something off its ear. "Anyway, I just
wanted to say how sorry I was."

"You're very kind," he says.

"It seems so senseless," she murmurs. "There's something so
senseless about it when it happens. My sister went through a
stop sign. She just didn't see it, I guess. But it wasn't a busy road
or anything. If she'd come along one second later or sooner
nothing would've happened. So senseless. Two people driving
two different cars coming along on two roads on a sunny afternoon and they come together like that. I mean—what're the
chances, really?"

He doesn't say anything.

"How's Brenda handling it?"

"She's strong," he says.

"I would've said that," the woman tells him. "Sometimes I
think the children take these things better than the adults do.
I remember when she first came to my class. She told everyone
in the first minute that she'd come from Oregon. That she was
living with her grandfather, and her mother was divorced.

"She was a baby when the divorce—when she moved here
from Oregon."

This seems to surprise the woman. "Really," she says, low.
"I got the impression it was recent for her. I mean, you know,
that she had just come from it all. It was all very vivid for her,
I remember that."

"She was a baby," he says. It's almost as if he were insisting
on it. He's heard this in his voice, and he wonders if she has,
too.

"Well," she says, "I always had a special place for Brenda.
I always thought she was very special. A very special little girl."

The PTA meeting is over, and Mr. Clayton is now standing

at the far door with the first of his charges. They're all lining up outside the door, and Mr. Clayton walks to the microphone to announce the program. The demonstration will commence with the mini-trampoline and the vaulting horse: a performance by the fifth- and sixth-graders. There will also be a break-dancing demonstration by the fourth-grade class.

"Here we go," the woman says. "My nephew's afraid of the mini-tramp."

"They shouldn't make them do these things," Brenda's grandfather says, with a passion that surprises him. He draws in a breath. "It's too hard," he says, loudly. He can't believe himself. "They shouldn't have to go through a thing like this."

"I don't know," she says vaguely, turning from him a little. He has drawn attention to himself. Others in the crowd are regarding him now—one, a man with a sparse red beard and wild red hair, looking at him with something he takes for agreement.

"It's too much," he says, still louder. "Too much to put on a child. There's just so much a child can take."

Someone asks gently for quiet.

The first child is running down the long mat to the mini-trampoline; it's a girl, and she times her jump perfectly, soars over the horse. One by one, other children follow. Mr. Clayton and another man stand on either side of the horse and help those who go over on their hands. Two or three go over without any assistance at all, with remarkable effortlessness and grace.

"Well," Brenda's kindergarden teacher says, "there's my nephew."

The boy hits the mini-tramp and does a perfect forward flip in the air over the horse, landing upright and then rolling forward in a somersault.

"Yea, Jack!" she cheers. "No sweat! Yea, Jackie boy!"

The boy trots to the other end of the room and stands with the others; the crowd is applauding. The last of the sixth-graders goes over the horse, and Mr. Clayton says into the microphone that the fifth-graders are next. It's Brenda who's next. She stands in the doorway, her cheeks flushed, her legs looking too heavy in the tights. She's rocking back and forth on the balls of her feet, getting ready. It grows quiet. Her arms swing slightly, back and forth, and now, just for a moment, she's looking at the crowd, her face hiding whatever she's feeling. It's as if she were merely curious as to who is out there, but he knows she's looking for him, searching the crowd for her grandfather, who stands on his toes, unseen against the far wall, stands there thinking his heart might break, lifting his hand to wave.

THE MAN
WHO KNEW
BELLE STARR

MCRAE PICKED UP A HITCHER on his way west. It was a young woman, carrying a paper bag and a leather purse, wearing jeans and a shawl—which she didn't take off, though it was more than ninety degrees out, and Mcrae had no air conditioning. He was driving an old Dodge Charger with a bad exhaust system, and one long crack in the wraparound windshield. He pulled over for her and she got right in, put the leather purse on the seat between them, and settled herself with the paper bag on her lap between her hands. He had just crossed into Texas.

"Where you headed," he said.

She said, "What about you?"

"Nevada, maybe."

"Why maybe?"

And that fast he was answering *her* questions. "I just got out of the Air Force," he told her, though this wasn't exactly true. The Air Force had put him out with a dishonorable discharge after four years at Leavenworth for assaulting a staff sergeant. He was a bad character. He had a bad temper that had got him into a load of trouble already and he just wanted to get out west, out to the wide-open spaces. It was just to see it, really. He had the feeling people didn't require as much from a person way out where there was that kind of room. He didn't have any family now. He had five thousand dollars from his father's insurance policy, and he was going to make the money last him awhile. He said, "I'm sort of undecided about a lot of things."

"Not me," she said.

"You figured out where you were going," he said.

"You could say that."

"So where might that be."

She made a fist and then extended her thumb, and turned it over. "Under," she said; "down."

"Excuse me?"

"Does the radio work?" she asked, reaching for it.

"It's on the blink," he said.

She turned the knob anyway, then sat back and folded her arms over the paper bag.

He took a glance at her. She was skinny and long-necked, and her hair was the color of water in a metal pail. She looked just old enough for high school.

"What's in the bag?" he said.

She sat up a little. "Nothing. Another blouse."

"Well, so what did you mean back there?"

"Back where?"

"Look," he said, "we don't have to do any talking if you don't want to."

"Then what will we do?"

"Anything you want," he said.

"What if I just want to sit here and let you drive me all the way to Nevada?"

"That's fine," he said. "That's just fine."

"Well, I won't do that. We can talk."

"Are *you* going to Nevada?" he asked.

She gave a little shrug of her shoulders. "Why not?"

"All right," he said, and for some reason he offered her his hand. She looked at it, and then smiled at him, and he put his hand back on the wheel.

• • •

IT got a little awkward almost right away. The heat was awful, and she sat there sweating, not saying much. He never thought he was very smooth or anything, and he had been in prison: it had been a long time since he had found himself in the company of a woman. Finally she fell asleep, and for a few miles he could look at her without worrying about anything but staying on the road. He decided that she was kind of good-looking around the eyes and mouth. If she ever filled out, she might be something. He caught himself wondering what might happen, thinking of sex. A girl who traveled alone like this was probably pretty loose. Without quite realizing it, he began to daydream about her, and when he got aroused by the daydream he tried to concentrate on figuring his chances, playing his cards right, not messing up any opportunities—but being gentlemanly, too. He was not the sort of person who forced himself on young women. She slept very quietly, not breathing loudly or sighing or moving much; and then she simply sat up and folded her arms over the bag again and stared out at the road.

"God," she said, "I went out."

"You hungry?" he asked.

"No."

"What's your name?" he said. "I never got your name."

"Belle Starr," she said, and, winking at him, she made a clicking sound out of the side of her mouth.

"Belle Starr," he said.

"Don't you know who Belle Starr was?"

All he knew was that it was a familiar-sounding name. "Belle Starr."

She put her index finger to the side of his head and said, "Bang."

"Belle Starr," he said.

"Come on," she said. "Annie Oakley. Wild Bill Hickok."

"Oh," Mcrae said. "Okay."

"That's me," she said, sliding down in the seat. "Belle Starr."

"That's not your real name."

"It's the only one I go by these days."

They rode on in silence for a time.

"What's *your* name?" she said.

He told her.

"Irish?"

"I never thought about it."

"Where you from, Mcrae?"

"Washington, D.C."

"Long way from home."

"I haven't been there in years."

"Where *have* you been?"

"Prison," he said. He hadn't known he would say it, and now that he had, he kept his eyes on the road. He might as well have been posing for her; he had an image of himself as he must look from the side, and he shifted his weight a little, sucked in his belly. When he stole a glance at her he saw that she was simply gazing out at the Panhandle, one hand up like a visor to shade her eyes.

"What about you?" he said, and felt like somebody in a movie —two people with a past come together on the open road. He wondered how he could get the talk around to the subject of love.

"What *about* me?"

"Where're you from?"

"I don't want to bore you with all the facts," she said.

"I don't mind," Mcrae said. "I got nothing else to do."

"I'm from way up North."

"Okay," he said, "you want me to guess?"

"Maine," she said. "Land of Moose and Lobster."

He said, "Maine. Well, now."

"See?" she said. "The facts are just a lot of things that don't change."

"Unless you change them," Mcrae said.

She reached down and, with elaborate care, as if it were fragile, put the paper bag on the floor. Then she leaned back and put her feet up on the dash. She was wearing low-cut tennis shoes.

"You going to sleep?" he asked.

"Just relaxing," she said.

But a moment later, when he asked if she wanted to stop and eat, she didn't answer, and he looked over to see that she was sound asleep.

His father had died while he was at Leavenworth. The last time Mcrae saw him, he was lying on a gurney in one of the bays of D.C. General's emergency ward, a plastic tube in his mouth, an I.V. set into an ugly yellow-blue bruise on his wrist. Mcrae had come home on leave from the Air Force—which he had joined at the order of a juvenile judge—to find his father on the floor in the living room, in a pile of old newspapers and bottles, wearing his good suit, with no socks or shoes and no shirt. It looked as if he were dead. But the ambulance drivers found a pulse, and rushed him off to the hospital. Mcrae cleaned the house up a little, and then followed in the Charger. The old man had been steadily going downhill from the time Mcrae was a boy, and so this latest trouble wasn't new. In the hospital, they got the tube into his mouth and hooked him to the I.V., and then left him there on the gurney. Mcrae stood at his side, still in uniform, and when the old man opened his eyes and looked at him it was clear that he didn't know who it was. The old man blinked, stared, and then sat up, took the tube out of his mouth, and spat something terrible-looking into a small metal dish which was suspended from the complicated apparatus of the room, and which made a continual water-dropping sound like a leaking sink. He looked at Mcrae again, and then he looked at the tube. "Jesus Christ," he said.

"Hey," Mcrae said.

"What."

"It's me."

The old man put the tube back into his mouth and looked away.

"Pops," Mcrae said. He didn't feel anything.

The tube came out. "Don't look at me, boy. You got yourself into it. Getting into trouble, stealing and running around. You got yourself into it."

"I don't mind it, Pops. It's three meals and a place to sleep."

"Yeah," the old man said, and then seemed to gargle something. He spit into the little metal dish again.

"I got thirty days of leave, Pops."

"Eh?"

"I don't have to go back for a month."

"Where you going?"

"Around," Mcrae said.

The truth was that he hated the Air Force, and he was thinking of taking the Charger and driving to Canada or someplace like that, and hiding out the rest of his life—the Air Force felt like punishment, it *was* punishment, and he had already been in trouble for his quick temper and his attitude. That afternoon, he'd left his father to whatever would happen, got into the Charger, and started north. But he hadn't made it. He'd lost heart a few miles south of New York City, and he turned around and came back. The old man had been moved to a room in the alcoholic ward, but Mcrae didn't go to see him. He stayed in the house, watching television and drinking beer, and when old high school buddies came by he went around with them a little. Mostly he stayed home, though, and at the end of his leave he locked the place and drove back to Chanute, in Illinois, where he was stationed. He wasn't there two months before the staff sergeant caught him drinking beer in the dayroom of one of the training barracks, and asked for his name. Mcrae walked over to him, said, "My name is trouble," and at the word *trouble,* struck the other man in the face. He'd had a lot of the beer, and he had been sitting there in the dark, drinking the last of it, going over everything in his mind, and the staff sergeant, a baby-faced man with a spare tire of flesh around his waist and an attitude about the stripes on his sleeves, had just walked into it. Mcrae didn't even know him. Yet he stood over the sergeant where he had fallen, and then started kicking him. It took two other men to get him off the poor man, who wound up in the hospital with a broken jaw (the first punch had done it), a few cracked ribs, and multiple lacerations and bruises. The court-martial was swift. The sentence was four years at hard labor, along with the dishonorable discharge. He'd had less than a month to go on the sentence when he got the news about his father. He felt no surprise, nor, really, any grief; yet there was a little thrill of something like fear: he was in his cell, and for an instant some part of him actually wanted to remain there, inside walls, where things were certain, and there weren't any decisions to make. A week later, he learned of the money from the insurance, which would have been more than the five thousand except that his father had been a few months behind on the rent, and on other payments. Mcrae settled what he had to of those things, and kept the rest. He had started to feel like a happy man, out of Leavenworth and the Air Force, and now he was on his way to Nevada, or someplace like that—and he had picked up a girl.

He drove on until dusk, stopping only for gas, and the girl slept right through. Just past the line into New Mexico, he pulled off the interstate and went north for a mile or so, looking for some place other than a chain restaurant to eat. She sat up straight, pushed the hair back away from her face. "Where are we?"

"New Mexico," he said. "I'm looking for a place to eat."

"I'm not hungry."

"Well," he said, "*you* might be able to go all day without anything to eat, but I got a three-meal-a-day habit to support."

She brought the paper bag up from the floor and held it in her lap.

"You got food in there?" he asked.

"No."

"You're very pretty—child-like, sort of—when you sleep."

"I didn't snore?"

"You were quiet as a mouse."

"And you think I'm pretty."

"I guess you know a thing like that. I hope I didn't offend you."

"I don't like dirty remarks," she said. "But I don't guess you meant to be dirty."

"Dirty."

"Sometimes people can say a thing like that and mean it very dirty, but I could tell you didn't."

He pulled in at a roadside diner and turned off the ignition. "Well?" he said.

She sat there with the bag on her lap. "I don't think I'll go in with you."

"You can have a cold drink or something," he said.

"You go in. I'll wait out here."

"Come on in there with me and have a cold drink," Mcrae said. "I'll buy it for you. I'll buy you dinner if you want."

"I don't want to," she said.

He got out and started for the entrance, and before he reached it he heard her door open and close, and turned to watch her come toward him, thin and waif-like in the shawl, which hid her arms and hands.

The diner was empty. There was a long, low bar, with soda fountains on the other side of it, and glass cases in which pies and cakes were set. There were booths along one wall. Everything seemed in order, except that no one was around. Mcrae and the girl stood in the doorway for a moment and waited, and finally she stepped in and took a seat in the first booth. "I guess we're supposed to seat ourselves," she said.

"This is weird," said Mcrae.

"Hey," she said, rising, "there's a jukebox." She strode over to it and leaned on it, crossing one leg behind the other at the ankle, her hair falling down to hide her face.

"Hello?" Mcrae said. "Anybody here?"

"Got any change?" asked the girl.

He gave her a quarter, and then sat at the bar. The door at the far end swung in, and a big, red-faced man entered, wearing a white cook's apron over a sweat-stained baby-blue shirt, whose sleeves he had rolled up past the meaty curve of his elbows. "Yeah?" he said.

"You open?" Mcrae asked.

"That jukebox don't work, honey," the man said.

"You open?" Mcrae said, as the girl came and sat down beside him.

"Sure, why not?"

"Place is kind of empty."

"What do you want to eat?"

"You got a menu?"

"You want a menu?"

"Sure," Mcrae said, "why not?"

"Truth is," the big man said, "I'm selling this place. I don't have menus anymore. I make hamburgers and breakfast stuff. Some french fries and cold drinks. A hot dog maybe. I'm not keeping track."

"Let's go somewhere else," the girl said.

"Yeah," said the big man, "why don't you do that."

"Look," said Mcrae, "what's the story here?"

The other man shrugged. "You came in at the end of the run, you know what I mean? I'm going out of business. Sit down and I'll make you a hamburger on the house."

Mcrae looked at the girl.

"Okay," she said, in a tone which made it clear that she would've been happier to leave.

The big man put his hands on the bar and leaned toward her.

"Miss, if I were you I wouldn't look a gift horse in the mouth."

"I don't like hamburger," she said.

"You want a hot dog?" the man said. "I got a hot dog for you. Guaranteed to please."

"I'll have some french fries," she said.

The big man turned to the grill and opened the metal drawer under it. He was very wide at the hips, and his legs were like trunks. "I get out of the Army after twenty years," he said, "and I got a little money put aside. The wife and I decide we want to get into the restaurant business. The government's going to be paying me a nice pension and we got the savings, so we sink it all in this goddamn diner. Six and a half miles from the interstate. You get the picture? The guy's selling us this diner at a great price, you know? A terrific price. For a song, I'm in the restaurant business. The wife will cook the food, and I'll wait tables, you know, until we start to make a little extra, and then we'll hire somebody—a high school kid or somebody like that. We might even open another restaurant if the going gets good enough. But of course, this is New Mexico. This is six and a half miles from the interstate. There's nothing here anymore because there's nothing up the road. You know what's up the road? Nothing." He had put the hamburger on, and a basket of frozen french fries. "Now the wife decides she's had enough of life on the border, and off she goes to Seattle to sit in the rain with her mother and here I am trying to sell a place nobody else is dumb enough to buy. You know what I mean?"

"That's rough," Mcrae said.

"You're the second customer I've had all *week*, bub."

The girl said, "I guess that cash register's empty then, huh."

"It ain't full, honey."

She got up and wandered across the room. For a while she stood gazing out the windows over the booths, her hands invisible under the woolen shawl. When she came back to sit next to Mcrae again, the hamburger and french fries were ready.

"On the house," the big man said.

And the girl brought a gun out of the shawl—a pistol that looked like a toy. "Suppose you open up that register, Mr. Poormouth," she said.

The big man looked at her, then at Mcrae, who had taken a large bite of his hamburger, and had it bulging in his cheeks.

"This thing is loaded, and I'll use it."

"Well for Christ's sake," the big man said.

Mcrae started to get off the stool. "Hold on a minute," he said to them both, his words garbled by the mouthful of food, and then everything started happening all at once. The girl aimed the pistol. There was a popping sound—a single, small pop, not much louder than the sound of a cap gun—and the big man took a step back, against the counter, into the dishes and pans there. He stared at the girl, wide-eyed, for what seemed a long time, then went down, pulling dishes with him in a tremendous shattering.

"Jesus Christ," Mcrae said, swallowing, standing back from her, raising his hands.

She put the pistol back in her jeans under the shawl, and then went around the counter and opened the cash register. "Damn," she said.

Mcrae said, low, "Jesus Christ."

And now she looked at him; it was as if she had forgotten he was there. "What're you standing there with your hands up like that?"

"God," he said, "oh, God."

"Stop it," she said. "Put your hands down."

He did so.

"Cash register's empty." She sat down on one of the stools and gazed over at the body of the man where it had fallen. "Damn."

"Look," Mcrae said, "take my car. You—you can have my car."

She seemed puzzled. "I don't want your car. What do I want your car for?"

"You—" he said. He couldn't talk, couldn't focus clearly, or think. He looked at the man, who lay very still, and then he began to cry.

"Will you stop it?" she said, coming off the stool, reaching under the shawl and bringing out the pistol again.

"Jesus," he said. "Good Jesus."

She pointed the pistol at his forehead. "Bang," she said. "What's my name?"

"Your—name?"

"My name."

"Belle—" he managed.

"Come on," she said. "The whole thing—you remember."

"Belle—Belle Starr."

"Right." She let the gun hand drop to her side, into one of the folds of the shawl. "I like that so much better than Annie Oakley."

"Please," Mcrae said.

She took a few steps away from him and then whirled and aimed the gun. "I think we better get out of here, what do you think?"

"Take the car," he said, almost with exasperation; it frightened him to hear it in his own voice.

"I can't drive," she said simply. "Never learned."

"Jesus," he said. It went out of him like a sigh.

"God," she said, gesturing with the pistol for him to move to the door, "it's hard to believe you were ever in *prison.*"

THE road went on into the dark, beyond the fan of the headlights; he lost track of miles, road signs, other traffic, time; trucks came by and surprised him, and other cars seemed to materialize as they started the lane change that would bring them over in front of him. He watched their taillights grow small in the distance, and all the while the girl sat watching him, her hands somewhere under the shawl. For a long time there was just the sound of the rushing night air at the windows, and then she moved a little, shifted her weight, bringing one leg up on the seat.

"What were you in prison for, anyway?"

Her voice startled him, and for a moment he couldn't think to answer.

"Come on," she said, "I'm getting bored with all this quiet. What were you in prison for?"

"I—beat up a guy."

"That's all?"

"Yes, that's all." He couldn't keep the irritation out of his voice.

"Tell me about it."

"It was just—I just beat up a guy. It wasn't anything."

"I didn't shoot that man for money, you know."

Mcrae said nothing.

"I shot him because he made a nasty remark to me about the hot dogs."

"I didn't hear any nasty remark."

"He shouldn't have said it or else he'd still be alive."

Mcrae held tight to the wheel.

"Don't you wish it was the Wild West?" she said.

"Wild West," he said, "yeah." He could barely speak for the dryness in his mouth and the deep ache of his own breathing.

"You know," she said, "I'm not really from Maine."

He nodded.

"I'm from Florida."

"Florida," he managed.

"Yes, only I don't have a Southern accent, so people think I'm not from there. Do you hear any trace of a Southern accent at all when I talk?"

"No," he said.

"Now you—you've got an accent. A definite Southern accent."

He was silent.

"Talk to me," she said.

"What do you want me to say?" he said. "Jesus."

"You could ask me things."

"Ask you things—"

"Ask me what my name is."

Without hesitating, Mcrae said, "What's your name?"

"You know."

"No, really," he said, trying to play along.

"It's Belle Starr."

"Belle Starr," he said.

"Nobody *but,*" she said.

"Good," he said.

"And I don't care about money, either," she said. "That's not what I'm after."

"No," Mcrae said.

"What I'm after is adventure."

"Right," said Mcrae.

"Fast living."

"Fast living, right."

"A good time."

"Good," he said.

"I'm going to live a ton before I die."

"A ton, yes."

"What about you?" she said.

"Yes," he said. "Me too."

"Want to join up with me?"

"Join up," he said. "Right." He was watching the road.

She leaned toward him a little. "Do you think I'm lying about my name?"

"No."

"Good," she said.

He had begun to feel as though he might start throwing up what he'd had of the hamburger. His stomach was cramping on him, and he was dizzy. He might even be having a heart attack.

"Your eyes are big as saucers," she said.

He tried to narrow them a little. His whole body was shaking now.

"You know how old I am, Mcrae? I'm nineteen."

He nodded, glanced at her and then at the road again.

"How old are you?"

"Twenty-three."

"Do you believe people go to heaven when they die?"

"Oh, God," he said.

"Look, I'm not going to shoot you while you're driving the car. We'd crash if I did that."

"Oh," he said. "Oh, Jesus, please—look. I never saw anybody shot before—"

"Will you *stop it*?"

He put one hand to his mouth. He was soaked; he felt the sweat on his upper lip, and then he felt the dampness all through his clothes.

She said, "I don't kill everybody I meet, you know."

"No," he said. "Of course not." The absurdity of this exchange almost brought a laugh up out of him. It was astonishing that such a thing as a laugh could be anywhere in him at such a time, but here it was, rising up in his throat like some loosened part of his anatomy. He held on with his whole mind, and it was a moment before he realized that *she* was laughing.

"Actually," she said, "I haven't killed all that many people."

"How—" he began. Then he had to stop to breathe. "How many?"

"Take a guess."

"I don't have any idea," he said.

"Well," she said, "you'll just have to guess. And you'll notice that I haven't spent any time in prison."

He was quiet.

"*Guess,*" she said.

Mcrae said, "Ten?"

"No."

He waited.

"Come on, keep guessing."

"More than ten?"

"Maybe."

"More than ten," he said.

"Well, all right. Less than ten."

"Less than ten," he said.

"Guess," she said.

"Nine."

"No."

"Eight."

"No, not eight."

"Six?"

"Not six."

"Five?"

"Five and a half people," she said. "You almost hit it right on the button."

"Five and a half people," said Mcrae.

"Right. A kid who was hitchhiking, like me; a guy at a gas station; a dog that must've got lost—I count him as the half—another guy at a gas station; a guy that took me to a motel and made an obscene gesture to me; and the guy at the diner. That makes five and a half."

"Five and a half," Mcrae said.

"You keep repeating everything I say. I wish you'd quit that."

He wiped his hand across his mouth and then feigned a cough to keep from having to speak.

"Five and a half people," she said, turning a little in the seat, putting her knees up on the dash. "Have you ever met anybody like me? Tell the truth."

"No," Mcrae said, "nobody."

"Just think about it, Mcrae. You can say you rode with Belle Starr. You can tell your grandchildren."

He was afraid to say anything to this, for fear of changing the delicate balance of the thought. Yet he knew the worst mistake would be to say nothing at all. He was beginning to feel something of the cunning that he would need to survive, even as he knew the slightest miscalculation would mean the end of him. He said, with fake wonder, "I knew Belle Starr."

She said, "Think of it."

"Something," he said.

And she sat further down in the seat. "Amazing."

HE kept to fifty-five miles an hour, and everyone else was speeding. The girl sat straight up now, nearly facing him on the seat. For long periods she had been quiet, simply watching him drive, and soon they were going to need gas. There was now less than half a tank.

"Look at these people speeding," she said. "We're the only ones obeying the speed limit. Look at them."

"Do you want me to speed up?" he asked.

"I think they ought to get tickets for speeding, that's what I think. Sometimes I wish I was a policeman."

"Look," Mcrae said, "we're going to need gas pretty soon."

"No, let's just run it until it quits. We can always hitch a ride with somebody."

"This car's got a great engine," Mcrae said. "We might have to outrun the police, and I wouldn't want to do that in any other car."

"This old thing? It's got a crack in the windshield. The radio doesn't work."

"Right. But it's a fast car. It'll outrun a police car."

She put one arm over the seat back and looked out the rear window. "You really think the police are chasing us?"

"They might be," he said.

She stared at him a moment. "No. There's no reason. Nobody saw us."

"But if somebody did—this car, I mean, it'll go like crazy."

"I'm afraid of speeding, though," she said. "Besides, you know what I found out? If you run slow enough the cops go right past you. Right on past you looking for somebody who's in a hurry. No, I think it's best if we just let it run until it quits and then get out and hitch."

Mcrae thought he knew what might happen when the gas ran out: she would make him push the car to the side of the road, and then she would walk him back into the cactus and brush there, and when they were far enough from the road, she would shoot him. He knew this as if she had spelled it all out, and he began again to try for the cunning he would need. "Belle," he said. "Why don't we lay low for a few days in Albuquerque?"

"Is that an obscene gesture?" she said.

"No!" he said, almost shouted. "No! That's—it's outlaw talk. You know. Hide out from the cops—lay low. It's—it's prison talk."

"Well, I've never been in prison."

"That's all I meant."

"You want to hide out."

"Right," he said.

"You and me?"

"You—you asked if I wanted to join up with you."

"Did I?" She seemed puzzled by this.

"Yes," he said, feeling himself press it a little. "Don't you remember?"

"I guess I do."

"You did," he said.

"I don't know."

"Belle Starr had a gang," he said.

"She did."

"I could be the first member of your gang."

She sat there thinking this over. Mcrae's blood moved at the thought that she was deciding whether or not he would live. "Well," she said, "maybe."

"You've got to have a gang, Belle."

"We'll see," she said.

A moment later, she said, "How much money do you have?"

"I have enough to start a gang."

"It takes money to start a gang?"

"Well—" He was at a loss.

"How much do you have?"

He said, "A few hundred."

"Really?" she said. "That much?"

"Just enough to—just enough to get to Nevada."

"Can I have it?"

He said, "Sure." He was holding the wheel and looking out into the night.

"And we'll be a gang?"

"Right," he said.

"I like the idea. Belle Starr and her gang."

Mcrae started talking about what the gang could do, making it up as he went along, trying to sound like all the gangster movies he'd seen. He heard himself talking about things like robbery and getaway and staying out of prison, and then, as she sat there staring at him, he started talking about being at Leavenworth, what it was like. He went on about it, the hours of forced work, and the time alone; the harsh day-to-day routines, the bad food. Before he was through, feeling the necessity of deepening her sense of him as her new accomplice—and feeling strangely as though in some way he had indeed become exactly that—he was telling her everything, all the bad times he'd had: his father's alcoholism, and growing up wanting to hit something for the anger that was in him; the years of getting into trouble; the fighting and the kicking and what it had got him. He embellished it all, made it sound worse than it really was because she seemed to be going for it, and because, telling it to her, he felt oddly sorry for himself; a version of this story of pain and neglect and lonely rage was true. He had been through a lot. And as he finished, describing for her the scene at the hospital the last time he saw his father, he was almost certain that he had struck a chord in her. He thought he saw it in the rapt expression on her face.

"Anyway," he said, and smiled at her.

"Mcrae?" she said.

"Yeah?"

"Can you pull over?"

"Well," he said, his voice shaking, "why don't we wait until it runs out of gas?"

She was silent.

"We'll be that much further down the road," he said.

"I don't really want a gang," she said. "I don't like dealing with other people that much. I mean I don't think I'm a leader."

"Oh, yes," Mcrae said. "No—you're a leader. You're definitely a leader. I was in the Air Force and I know leaders and you are definitely what I'd call a leader."

"Really?"

"Absolutely. You are leadership material all the way."

"I wouldn't have thought so."

"Definitely," he said, "Definitely a leader."

"But I don't really like people around, you know."

"That's a leadership quality. Not wanting people around. It is definitely a leadership quality."

"Boy," she said, "the things you learn."

He waited. If he could only think himself through to the way out. If he could get her to trust him, get the car stopped—be there when she turned her back.

"You want to be in my gang, huh?"

"I sure do," he said.

"Well, I guess I'll have to think about it."

"I'm surprised nobody's mentioned it to you before."

"You're just saying that."

"No, really."

"Were you ever married?" she asked.

"Married?" he said, and then stammered over the answer. "Ah—uh, no."

"You ever been in a gang before?"

"A couple times, but—but they never had good leadership."

"You're giving me a line, huh."

"No," he said, "it's true. No good leadership. It was always a problem."

"I'm tired," she said, shifting toward him a little. "I'm tired of talking."

The steering wheel was hurting the insides of his hands. He held tight, looking at the coming-on of the white stripes in the road. There were no other cars now, and not a glimmer of light anywhere beyond the headlights.

"Don't you get tired of talking, sometimes?"

"I never was much of a talker," he said.

"I guess I don't mind talking as much as I mind listening," she said.

He made a sound in his throat that he hoped she took for agreement.

"That's just when I'm tired, though."

"Why don't you take a nap," he said.

She leaned back against the door and regarded him. "There's plenty of time for that later."

"So," he wanted to say, "you're not going to kill me—we're a gang?"

They had gone for a long time without speaking, a nerve-wrecking hour of minutes, during which the gas gauge had sunk to just above empty; and finally she had begun talking about herself, mostly in the third person. It was hard to make sense of most of it. Yet he listened as if to instructions concerning how to extricate himself. She talked about growing up in Florida, in the country, and owning a horse; she remembered when she was taught to swim by somebody she called Bill, as if Mcrae would know who that was; and then she told him how when her father ran away with her mother's sister, her mother started having men friends over all the time. "There was a lot of obscene goings-on," she said, and her voice tightened a little.

"Some people don't care what happens to their kids," said Mcrae.

"Isn't it the truth?" she said. Then she took the pistol out of the shawl. "Take this exit."

He pulled onto the ramp and up an incline to a two-lane road that went off through the desert, toward a glow that burned on the horizon. For perhaps five miles the road was straight as a plumb line, and then it curved into long, low undulations of sand and mesquite and cactus.

"My mother's men friends used to do whatever they wanted to me," she said. "It went on all the time. All sorts of obscene goings-on."

Mcrae said, "I'm sorry that happened to you, Belle." And for an instant he was surprised by the sincerity of his feeling: it was as if he couldn't feel sorry enough. Yet it was genuine: it all had to do with his own unhappy story. The whole world seemed very, very sad to him. "I'm really very sorry," he said.

She was quiet a moment, as if thinking about this. Then she said, "Let's pull over now. I'm tired of riding."

"It's almost out of gas," he said.

"I know, but pull it over anyway."

"You sure you want to do that?"

"See?" she said. "That's what I mean. I wouldn't like being told what I should do all the time, or asked if I was sure of what I wanted or not."

He pulled the car over and slowed to a stop. "You're right," he said, "See? Leadership. I'm just not used to somebody with leadership qualities."

She held the gun a little toward him. He was looking at the small, dark, perfect circle of the end of the barrel. "I guess we should get out, huh," she said.

"I guess so." He hadn't even heard himself.

"Do you have any relatives left anywhere?" she said.

"No."

"Your folks are both dead?"

"Right, yes."

"Which one died first?"

"I told you," he said, "didn't I? My mother. My mother died first."

"Do you feel like an orphan?"

He sighed. "Sometimes." The whole thing was slipping away from him.

"I guess I do too." She reached back and opened her door. "Let's get out now." And when he opened his door she aimed the gun at his head. "Get out slow."

"Aw, Jesus," he said. "Look, you're not going to do this, are you? I mean I thought we were friends and all."

"Just get out real slow, like I said to."

"Okay," he said, "I'm getting out." He opened his door, and the ceiling light surprised and frightened him. Some wordless part of himself understood that this was it, and all his talk had come to nothing: all the questions she had asked him, and everything he had told her—it was all completely useless. This was going to happen to him, and it wouldn't mean anything; it would just be what happened.

"Real slow," she said. "Come on."

"Why are you doing this?" he said. "You've got to tell me that before you do it."

"Will you please get out of the car now?"

He just stared at her.

"All right, I'll shoot you where you sit."

"Okay," he said, "don't shoot."

She said in an irritable voice, as though she were talking to a recalcitrant child, "You're just putting it off."

He was backing himself out, keeping his eyes on the little barrel of the gun, and he could hear something coming, seemed to notice it in the same instant that she said, "Wait." He stood half in and half out of the car, doing as she said, and a truck came over the hill ahead of them, a tractor-trailer, all white light and roaring.

"Stay still," she said, crouching, aiming the gun at him.

The truck came fast, was only fifty yards away, and without having to decide about it, without even knowing that he would do it, Mcrae bolted into the road. He was running: there was the exhausted sound of his own breath, the truck horn blaring, coming on, louder, the thing bearing down on him, something buzzing past his head. Time slowed. His legs faltered under him, were heavy, all the nerves gone out of them. In the light of the oncoming truck, he saw his own white hands outstretched as if to grasp something in the air before him, and then the truck was past him, the blast of air from it propelling him over the side of the road and down an embankment in high, dry grass, which pricked his skin and crackled like hay.

He was alive. He lay very still. Above him was the long shape of the road, curving off in the distance, the light of the truck going on. The noise faded and was nothing. A little wind stirred. He heard the car door close. Carefully, he got to all fours, and crawled a few yards away from where he had fallen. He couldn't be sure of which direction—he only knew he couldn't stay where he was. Then he heard what he thought were her footsteps in the road, and he froze. He lay on his side, facing the embankment. When she appeared there, he almost cried out.

"Mcrae? Did I get you?" She was looking right at where he was in the dark, and he stopped breathing. "Mcrae?"

He watched her move along the edge of the embankment.

"Mcrae?" She put one hand over her eyes, and stared at a place a few feet over from him; then she turned and went back out of sight. He heard the car door again, and again he began to crawl farther away. The ground was cold and rough, and there was a lot of sand.

He heard her put the key in the trunk, and he stood up, began to run, he was getting away, but something went wrong in his leg, something sent him sprawling, and a sound came out of him that seemed to echo, to stay on the air, as if to call her to him. He tried to be perfectly still, tried not to breathe, hearing now the small pop of the gun. He counted the reports: one, two, three. She was just standing there at the edge of the road, firing into the dark, toward where she must have thought she heard the sound. Then she was rattling the paper bag, reloading. He could hear the click of the gun. He tried to get up, and couldn't. He had sprained his ankle, had done something very bad to it. Now he was crawling wildly, blindly through the tall grass, hearing again the small report of the pistol. At last he rolled into a shallow gully, and lay there with his face down, breathing the dust, his own voice leaving him in a whimpering animal-like sound that he couldn't stop, even as he held both shaking hands over his mouth.

"Mcrae?" She sounded so close. "Hey," she said. "Mcrae?"

He didn't move. He lay there, perfectly still, trying to stop himself from crying. He was sorry for everything he had ever done. He didn't care about the money, or the car or going out west or anything. When he lifted his head to peer over the lip of the gully, and saw that she had started down the embankment with his flashlight, moving like someone with time and the patience to use it, he lost his sense of himself as Mcrae: he was just something crippled and breathing in the dark, lying flat in a little winding gully of weeds and sand. Mcrae was gone, was someone far, far away, from ages ago—a man fresh out of prison, with the whole country to wander in, and insurance money in his pocket, who had headed west with the idea that maybe his luck, at long last, had changed.

SPIRITS

I

I MET BROOKER AT ONE OF THOSE PARTIES for new faculty. I was just out of graduate school, after a stint in the Army, and I had just arrived, that July, to get myself ready for the fall semester. Brooker was the most distinguished member of the faculty, and I think I must've been surprised to see him. When I had come through on my campus interview in the spring, the people who squired me from place to place gave me the impression that he was notoriously aloof; there were bets among them as to who would next catch a glimpse of the creature.

But then, I was a fiction writer, the first ever hired to teach at this small, rather conservative teachers' college, and he wanted to get a look at me. He told me this in the first minute of our acquaintance, as if he wanted me to know he wasn't a regular at such gatherings: he really had come specifically to meet me. He had seen my stories in the magazines; he knew I had a book coming out, and he liked everything of mine that he'd seen. I was, of course, immediately and wholeheartedly in thrall. Remember that I was only twenty-six, and I suppose I offer this as an explanation, if not as an excuse; it could never have occurred to me then that he was merely flattering me.

The party took place on the lawn of the president's house, which was a two-hundred-year-old Colonial mansion with walls two feet thick and new, polished tile floors that shone unnaturally and made me think of carcinogens, for some reason. The president was a small, frail-looking old man with a single tuft of cottony white hair at the crown of his head, and twin tufts above his ears. His name was Keller, and he was a retired military officer with a Ph.D. in modern political history, Brooker told me. Dr. Keller was clearly delighted that Brooker had decided to attend his party. He stood in the open door to his house, the hallway shining behind him in a long perspective toward other open doors, and offered me his hand. "Come right through and get something else to drink, young man," he said. We had all been filing toward him from the lawn, which was dry and burned where there was no shade, and lush green under the willows and oaks and sycamores that surrounded the house.

"This is our writer," Brooker said to him.

"Well, and what do you write?"

"He writes stories, Dr. Keller."

"Oh. What kind of stories?"

Brooker left me to answer this, and I stammered something about seriousness that I'm sure Dr. Keller took as evidence of the folly of the English Department in having hired me in the first place. His next question was a clear indication of this.

"Are you tenure-track?"

"Yes, I am."

He nodded, and then he had turned to Brooker. They stood there exchanging comments about the turnout, the weather, the long spell without rain that had killed the grass, and I took this opportunity to study Brooker. For a man of nearly sixty, he was remarkably youthful-looking. His hair was gray, but thick, and his face still had the firm look of the face in the photographs of Brooker with Jack Kennedy before he ran for the presidency, or with Robert Kennedy near the end, or, later, with Lyndon Johnson. I remembered reading that Brooker had become disaffected with public service after the riots in Chicago, and had joined the faculty of a small private college in Virginia, and I was a little pie-eyed about the fact that I too was joining the faculty of that college. Life was roomy and full of possibility and promise; and I was for the moment quite simple and happy.

"So," Brooker said to me, entering the hall where I stood, "you have met our fine old president in his fine old house."

"Very nice," I said, gazing at the walls, the paintings there, which were of Virginia country scenes of a century ago.

"Have you found a place to live yet?"

I was paying a weekly rate at the Sweeney Motel off the interstate. I had paid the first month's deposit to rent a house that wouldn't be ready until the first week in September, and I was using the advance money on my book to make it until then. My wife had remained behind at the large Midwestern school where I had taken my degree; she would make her way here as soon as things were settled. I told him all this, feeling a little silly as I went on but finding myself unable to stop; it was information he seemed glad to have, and yet I wondered what could possibly interest him in it. I wound up talking about Mrs. Sweeney, who, because I was the same age as her son, had given me the single-room rate for a double, and kept stopping by to see me in the evenings, as if to give to the general pool of the world's kindness in the hope that somewhere someone else would offer something of it to her son.

"I'm giving a series of lectures at Chautauqua Institution this August," Brooker said. "I hate to suggest that you leave Mrs. Sweeney, but I wonder if you might not want to use my apartment for the month. You'd save money that way, and you could get some work done."

I just stood there.

"It must be awful trying to work in a motel."

"Well," I said, "I haven't been working."

"I'm going to be gone right through the last week of the month, because I have to spend some time in New York City too."

The president joined us then, wanting to introduce some

people to Brooker, who nodded at them and was gracious and witty while I watched. There were two women in the group, one of them not much older than I, and as the president began to talk about the lack of rain and his garden, Brooker leaned toward me and, breathing the wine he had drunk, murmured something that I wasn't sure I could've heard correctly. I looked at him—he seemed to be awaiting a signal of agreement from me—and when I didn't respond he leaned close again, and, with a nod of his head in the direction of the younger of the two women, repeated himself. It was a phrase so nakedly obscene that I took a step back from him. He winked at me, then turned his charm in her direction, asking her if she liked the president's fine old house.

"Built in 1771," Dr. Keller said, looking at the ceiling as though the date might have been inscribed there.

"I love old houses," the young woman said. "That's what my field of study is. The American house."

Brooker offered her his hand and introduced himself, and then began an animated conversation with her about modern architecture. I stood there awhile, then moved off, through the hallway to the kitchen and out the door there. Some people were still on the lawn, but I went past them, to my car, feeling abruptly quite homesick and depressed. I drove around the college and through the town streets for a while, just trying to get the sense of where things were. The place my wife and I had rented was on the north end of town, in a group of old, run-down frame houses. Sitting in the idling car and gazing at it, I felt as though we had made a mistake. The place was really run-down. The porch steps sagged; it needed painting. I had agreed to fix the place up for a break in the amount of rent, and now the whole thing seemed like too much to have to do along with moving and starting a new job. I drove away feeling like someone leaving the scene of an accident.

When I got back to the motel, Mrs. Sweeney was waiting for

me, and talking to her made me feel even worse. I kept hearing what Brooker had murmured in my ear. Mrs. Sweeney sensed that something was bothering me, and she was mercifully anxious not to intrude, or impose. She stayed only a few minutes, and then quietly excused herself and went on her way.

I had showered and was getting into bed before I remembered that Brooker had offered me his apartment. I was ready to doubt that he could've been sincere, and even so, when I called my wife, I found myself mentioning that I might be spending August as a house-sitter for none other than William Brooker.

"Who's William Brooker," she said.

I said, "You know who he is, Elaine."

"I'm not impressed," she said.

We didn't speak for a few seconds. Then I said, "So, do you miss me?"

"I miss you."

"What're you doing right now?" I asked.

"Talking to you."

With a feeling of suppressed irritation, I said, "What've you been doing all day?"

"Studying."

"The faculty orientation party was no fun," I said, and I went on to tell her about Brooker's murmured obscenity. Part of me simply wanted to express what I had felt about it all evening—that while I might have uttered exactly the same thing at one time or another, in Brooker's mouth and under those circumstances it was somehow more brutal than I could ever have meant it in my life. But there was also, I'm sure, the sense that my shock and disbelief would appeal to her.

"That doesn't seem like such an unusual thing for one man to say to another," she said. "Was she attractive?"

"You didn't hear the way he said it, Elaine."

"Did he slobber or something?"

Now I felt foolish. "Elaine, do you want to talk tonight?"

"Don't be mad," she said. "It really just doesn't sound like such an awful thing to me."

"Well," I said, "you weren't there."

"Are you going to stay in his apartment?" she asked.

"I don't know—I guess it'll save us money," I said, feeling wrong now, convinced that the whole question was pointless; that Brooker hadn't been serious, or that I had misinterpreted a gesture of hospitality anyone else would have known how to give the polite—and expected—refusal to.

"Why don't you hang up and go to sleep?" Elaine said. "You sound so tired."

"What if I get this apartment," I said. "Will you come out sooner?" And in the silence that followed, I added, "You could come out August first."

She said, "I'm in summer school, remember?"

"All right," I said, "the second week of August, then."

"We'll see."

"What's to keep you from coming then, Elaine?"

"We didn't plan it that way," she said.

Later, after we'd hung up and I'd been unable to fall asleep, I put my pants and shirt on and went out for a walk. Mrs. Sweeney was sitting on her little concrete slab of a porch, with a paperback book in her lap and a flyswatter in one hand, her stockings rolled down to her ankles, her hair in a white bandanna. She glanced over at me and smiled, and then went back to her reading. I went on up the sidewalk in my bare feet, and stood near the exit from the interstate, thinking about the fact that I was married, and that tonight my marriage felt like an old one, though we had been together only a little more than a year.

II

ELAINE was trying to finish a master's degree in library science. The first time I saw her, she was wearing a swimsuit. I had just finished my first year of graduate school and was living in a small room above a garage, trying to write, and spending most of my afternoons at a lake a few miles west of the campus. There was a beach house and restaurant on the lake, one of those places whose floors are covered with the sand that people track in from the beach, and whose atmosphere is suffused with the smell of suntan lotion. I was sitting alone at the counter, eating a hot dog, and two young women walked in, looking like health itself, tan and lithe and graceful in their bikinis. They ordered ice cream cones and then walked to the back of the room to see what songs were on the jukebox. I sat gazing at them, as did the boy behind the counter—a high school kid with a lot of baby fat still on him, and with the funny round eyes of a natural clown. There wasn't anyone else in the place, and when the women strolled out finally, the boy put his hands down on the counter and let his head droop. "It's a tough job," he said, "but somebody's got to do it."

I laughed. We were for the moment in that exact state of agreement which may in fact be possible only between strangers. I got up and went out to the shaded part of the beach, where the two of them had settled at a picnic table. I had never done anything of the kind, but I was so struck by their beauty that I simply began speaking to them. I asked if they were students at the college and if they were going to summer school, and I asked how they liked the lake. They were polite, and they gave each other a few smiling, knowing glances, but we spent the rest of the afternoon together, and when I left them I asked to see them both again; it was all quite friendly, and we agreed to meet at a pizza parlor just off campus. That night, when I went there to meet them, only one of them showed up. This was Elaine. We had something to eat, and we went for a walk, and the odd thing to recall now is that I was a little disappointed that she, and not her friend, had come to meet me. I remember feeling a little guilty about this as the evening wore on and it became evident that Elaine and I were going to be seeing each other.

As it turned out, her friend was leaving school, and I never saw her again; but even so, there were nights in that first year of our marriage when I would wake up next to Elaine and wonder about the friend. It was never anything but my mind wandering through possibility, of course, and yet when I think of Brooker, of the events that followed upon our first encounter at the faculty orientation party, my own woolgathering makes me feel rooted to the ground through the soles of my feet.

HE phoned me early the next morning. I had been lying awake, thinking about calling Elaine, and when his call came through I thought it *was* Elaine. "I wondered what happened to you," he said.

I was vague. I think I was even a little standoffish. I said something about having things to do, errands to run.

"Listen," he said, "I wondered if you were still interested in house-sitting for me."

I hemmed and hawed a little, the thought having crossed my mind that I hadn't actually said I *was* interested; for some reason, now, accuracy seemed important: it was as if I might lose something to him if I allowed him to blur any of the lines between us.

He said, "I don't want to impose on you."

"No," I said, "really. I'm very glad you thought of me."

"You'd be doing me a favor," he said.

And so we agreed that I would come to the apartment for a drink that evening, at which time I could get a look at the place. His wife was arriving from New York in the afternoon, and if past experience meant anything at all she would not feel like entertaining a dinner guest; but a quiet, sociable drink was something else again.

"I could come another night," I said.

"No," he said after a pause, "tonight will be fine."

After we hung up, I went outside, and found Mrs. Sweeney hanging wash on a line in the yard.

"Have you looked at television this morning?" she said. "Did you see the news last night? You see that guy arrested for molesting that little girl?"

She didn't wait for me to answer.

"That's my ex-husband," she said. Her eyes were wide and frightened and tearful. "You believe that? My ex-husband." She turned to hang up a sheet, and I thought I heard her sniffle. "You think you know a person," she went on; she was looking at me now. "You live with a person and you think you know him—know the way he is. His—all the way to his soul. You think you understand a man's spirit when you look in his eyes and he's your live-in partner for three years. Three years," she said. "Do you believe it? And he was always the cleanest, nicest man you'd ever want to meet. Quiet and easy to get along with and sort of simple about things, and a good storyteller some-times, when he felt like it. A little slow about work, sure—but."

"Maybe he's innocent," I said.

She stopped what she was doing and gave me a look almost of pity, except that there was impatience and frustration in it, too. "He confessed," she said. "He confessed to the whole thing. Can you imagine what this'll do to my boy, a thousand miles away from home, on some boat in the ocean, hearing that his stepfather did a terrible thing like that and then *confessed* to it?"

"Maybe the news won't get to him," I said.

"Oh, it'll get to him. I'll write and tell him about it. It'll get to him, all right." She put her apron full of clothespins in the basket at her feet and walked over to me. "I should be getting something for you to eat."

"No," I said, "I'm fine."

"I have a cook named Clara, but she's sick."

She had told me this on the day I registered—she'd repeated

it three or four times since. I had begun to wonder what this Clara must be like to be missed so much.

"I'm fine," I told her.

She shook her head. "Do you believe it? A little girl." Then she turned and pointed at the motel office. "The paper's right inside the door there. It's on the front page if you want to read about it. My husband a rapist, for God's sake."

"It's a terrible thing," I said as she marched toward the office. I think she meant to get the newspaper and bring it out to me, but then the phone rang in my room, and she said over her shoulder that I could come see it when I had the time. I went back into the room, certain that the call was from Elaine. I said "Howdy" into the telephone, and was greeted with a silence. "Hello?" I said.

"Uh, yes. This is William Brooker. Listen, I wanted to ask you. . . ." There was another silence, during which he sighed, like someone backing down from something. "Look, this is a little embarrassing. I mean I suppose it could wait until tonight. But I'd had a few drinks before I—before the party, you see."

"Yes?" I said, trying to sound only politely interested.

"Well—I said something last night—you know. We were all standing there and that extremely choice young lady was talking to Dr. Keller, and—you remember I said something a little off-color to you . . ."

"I didn't quite hear what it was," I lied.

"Oh. Well, I was wondering if you thought the young lady might've heard me. Or Dr. Keller."

"I wouldn't be able to say for sure."

"Yes, well. I shouldn't bother you with it. You say you didn't hear it at all?"

"That's right."

"I don't like to offend," he said.

And I was suddenly seized with a perverse desire to make him repeat the phrase that had so unnerved me the night before. "What was it, anyway?" I asked him.

"Oh, nothing. Just something a little—a silly little comment, you know. A joke. An impolite little aside. What I'd like to do to her—that sort of thing."

"Well," I said, wanting just as suddenly to let him off the hook, "I'm sure no one heard you."

"But—you said you *couldn't* be sure." Precision was Brooker's talent, someone had said.

"I'm reasonably sure, Professor Brooker. I mean if *I* couldn't hear you I don't think anyone else could."

"That's right," he said. "Good." I had the feeling that I had just heard the tone he took in his classroom, leading a group of neophytes through the thicket of Twentieth-Century Politics.

"So," I said.

He said, "Well, I guess I'll see you tonight." Then, exactly as though it were an afterthought, he told me I ought to wear a suit and tie for the occasion.

"Excuse me?" I said.

"There'll be one or two other people here, if you don't mind."

"Not at all," I said. And I didn't really hear him as he talked about who his other guests would be, because I was thinking about the fact that I didn't have a suit *or* a tie, and so would have to go out and buy them. I had exactly twenty-two dollars in my pocket, and there was perhaps another forty in the checking account I'd opened only that week. The next installment of my advance wouldn't arrive for days.

Brooker had hung up before I could muster the courage to apprise him of this, and then I decided I wouldn't want him to know under any circumstances. I would simply go without if I had to.

Of course I knew I would do no such thing. I would probably have been willing to steal what I needed; but as it turned out this wasn't necessary. Mrs. Sweeney's son was about my height and build, and he had left four suits behind—this was apparently his whole stock of them—along with about five hundred ties, all given to *him* by his former stepfather, the rapist and child molester, who according to Mrs. Sweeney had had a thing about ties, had collected them like somebody hoarding a thing that would soon be rare and hard to get. I chose a plain blue one, and a gray suit. I tried the suit on, standing in Mrs. Sweeney's spare room, and it fit well enough. Mrs. Sweeney made me wait while she ironed my shirt, and then that evening, after I'd got myself dressed and ready to go, she fussed with me, straightened the tie and brushed my arms and shoulders, her boy, going off to his first party in town. It seemed the appropriate thing to kiss her on the cheek before I left, and I'm afraid I embarrassed her.

"Good Lord," she said, but then she squeezed my elbow.

I almost asked what time she wanted me home.

III

BROOKER'S directions were characteristically precise. I had given myself a few minutes to allow for any trouble finding the place, and so I was early. I walked up the sidewalk in front of the building, already feeling stiff and uncomfortable in my suit and my rapist's tie, and Brooker came out on the landing and called to me. He was in shirt sleeves, the sleeves rolled up past his wrists.

"So glad you could make it," he said.

By the time I got up to him he had rolled the sleeves down and was buttoning them.

"I guess I'm a little early."

He ushered me inside and offered me a drink. Anything I wanted. I told him I'd wait awhile, and he excused himself and went upstairs. I sat in the living room, in the middle of his white sofa, my hands on my thighs, my back ramrod-stiff. It wasn't the sort of room you could relax in. There was a fireplace, and a baby grand piano, and on every available surface there were figurines and cut-glass shapes and statuary. The chairs and the love seat and the ottoman were not in the sort of proximity that would make conversation very easy, and the wallpaper was of a dark red hue that was really rather gloomy. I remembered that I had come to look at the place, and in an odd shift of mind I had an image of me sitting there with the whole apartment to myself. Whatever else this room was, it was luxuriously appointed, and I knew I was going to enjoy the luxury of entering and leaving it as I pleased.

Now I sat back a little and breathed a satisfied sigh, while upstairs I heard Brooker and his wife moving around. Twice I heard her heels as she crossed from one room to another, and then she came down the stairs. She was a striking woman in her mid-forties, with wonderful square shoulders and deep, clear blue eyes, and she was wearing a white evening gown that made her skin look marvelously tan and smooth. She offered me her hand (I nearly brought it to my lips), and asked, in a voice that was warm and rich and full of humor, if I would come keep her company in the kitchen while she got things ready for the evening. Apart from being a little breathless at the sight of her, I was now beginning to wonder if I hadn't come more than a little early.

I said, "I must've got the time wrong, Mrs. Brooker."

"Call me Helen," she said, leading me into the kitchen. "And you shouldn't worry about being early—we're just running a little late."

The kitchen was a light-filled, high-ceilinged room that looked as though it might've been transported, brick by brick, board by board, from one of the family farms in Brooker's native Minnesota. She indicated that I was to sit at the table in the center of the room, and then began opening cabinets and hutches, bringing out dishes, glasses, boxes of crackers, knives and forks.

"Can I help?" I said.

"Absolutely not. I could never stand servants in the house because I wanted to do it all myself, and as you can see I can't even let a guest be polite without launching into an explanation of this—quirk of mine." She paused. "Do you like the kitchen?"

"It's a very nice room," I said.

"Well, and you're going to be calling it home, aren't you."

"For a month. I guess so."

She went about her work, slicing cheese, arranging crackers on the plates and making dip, and I sat watching her.

"William says your wife isn't with you."

"No."

"Too bad," she said. "Do you miss her?"

"Very much."

"William travels so much. It's just odd that we're both going this time."

"I'll take good care of things," I said.

She waved this away as if there could be no doubt about it, and then without asking what I wanted she fixed me a glass of bourbon on ice. "If this isn't to your taste I'll drink it myself."

"It's fine," I said, and she gave me an odd look, as though my answer had surprised her. I sipped the whiskey, and she went back to setting things in order for the evening's guests, who were apparently arriving now—we could hear Brooker greeting someone out in the hall.

"William will think I stole you from him," she said. "Do you mind if I have a sip of your drink? I don't really want to have a whole one."

I handed her my glass. She took a long, slow sip, then breathed. I have loved the taste of whiskey since I was very young and my father would take me out on the porch at home and let me sip it out of sight of my mother, and I have never seen anyone—nor, I believe, have I myself ever enjoyed a sip of whiskey as much as this stately and beautiful woman did that night in Brooker's kitchen.

"Very good," she said, and smiled, handing the glass back to me. There was something a little hurried about the way she did it, and then I realized that Brooker was coming down the hall.

I put the drink down on the table in front of me and tried to look calm as he entered the room, leading Dr. Keller, who did not remember having met me, and who, again, asked if I was tenure-track. We had got past all that and in the next moment Brooker asked his wife if she wanted a glass of bourbon.

"Not on your life," she said.

"I always ask and she always refuses," Brooker said. "I don't know if I like disciplined people."

"Why don't *you* have some?" she said to him.

"No," he said, "I'm off it, too."

Dr. Keller also declined, and so now I was the only person in the group who was drinking. I found this a little irritating, and I made up my mind that I was going to sip the drink very slowly; I might even ask for another. I sat watching Mrs. Brooker put the finishing touches on a plateful of cheeses and cold cuts, while the two men stood talking about diets and diet drinks. Their conversation seemed so banal that I wondered if they weren't trading sides of a sort of running joke, but they were serious: Brooker's full attention was on the college president as he listed his various reasons for preferring iced tea without sugar over the sugarless colas. And then I noticed something else. Helen Brooker was staring at me. She had finished with everything and was simply standing there with her legs crossed at the ankles, gazing at me with all the frankness of a child. When I turned a little and met her gaze, she smiled and offered to refresh my glass.

IT was an odd evening. The other guests arrived, two couples. They were people of Brooker's age and class, and Dr. Keller introduced the men as members of the Board of Visitors of the college.

"This is our writer," he said, presenting me to them. "Professor Brooker was so kind as to invite him here tonight."

The two men shook my hand, and their wives nodded at me

from the snowy expanse of the couch. I sat in one of the wing chairs near the fireplace and was promptly forgotten. Brooker had begun to hold forth about the Kennedy years, and I noticed that his wife sat staring at her nails while he talked. She had heard it all before, of course, and she was doing a bad job of disguising her boredom. Finally she got up and carried a couple of empty plates into the kitchen, and when she came back out she had a glass of whiskey. She sat down next to the wives, and when she crossed her legs and let her high-heeled shoe slip to the toe of the dangling foot, my blood jumped. I went into the kitchen to pour my own whiskey, and I think I entertained for a moment the rather puerile fancy that she would make her way to me there, and that she might confess something to me, something I could console her for. But no one came, and in a little while I carried my fresh drink back to the chair by the fireplace.

The others were all drinking iced tea from a tray on the coffee table. I sipped my drink, and watched Helen Brooker sip hers. The talk was general now, and very stilted and hesitant; there seemed no common history for any of them to talk about—or there *was* a common history that all of them were avoiding as a subject for talk. In any case, I grew very tired and so deeply bored that I may even have nodded off once or twice. When Mrs. Brooker stood to go fix herself another drink, I got up too. I meant to leave, but before I could make my apologies she took me by the arm and walked with me into the kitchen.

"You haven't really seen the place," she said.

"It's fine," I said.

"We keep our bourbon in here to discourage our guests." She was pouring it into her glass. "Billy doesn't like trying to talk to drunks."

"Billy."

"Brooker." She tipped her head slightly to the side. "Doesn't it sound like a little innocent boy: Billy Brooker? That's what they called him, you know."

"Who?" I said.

"The Kennedys."

"Did you know him then—when he was with the Kennedys?"

"I worked for him. I was his secretary."

"You must've been very young."

She took a sip of her drink. "Billy's thirteen years older than I am. He was forty-two and I was twenty-nine. I was just out of a very unhappy marriage, and of course he was—well, he was the famous Mr. Brooker, though I must say I was really in love with Jack Kennedy more than anything else. We were all in love with him—the whole staff. And of course I voted for him because I thought he was so handsome. A lot of women *and* men did that, you know."

"I wasn't old enough to vote, but I guess I would have," I said.

"You were fascinated with him." It was as though she were leading me toward something.

"I liked his speeches."

"He was an awful womanizer, you know."

"That's what they say."

"Are you a womanizer?" She smiled, swallowed some of her drink, turning to face her husband, who came into the room from the back door and stood for a moment, looking at her and then at me.

"Hogging the booze," he said.

"Here," said his wife, lazily handing him hers. "If I have any more I'll wind up with a headache."

"Cheers," Brooker said, and drank.

"Have our guests departed, Billy?"

"They've departed."

"I've got to go," I said.

"Why don't you have another drink?" Brooker said. "You haven't really seen the place yet."

So I stayed for another glass of bourbon, which was enough to make me a little bleary-eyed and giddy for the drive back to the motel. Brooker walked me through the upstairs rooms of the apartment, including his wife's reading room, as he called it (it looked like a bedroom), and his study. She excused herself and went off to another room to bed, leaving the smell of her perfume everywhere.

"Your wife is very beautiful," I said to him when she had gone.

"Yes," he said as if we had agreed on something quite unimportant.

The upstairs rooms were spacious and comfortable-looking, and there was a television room I knew I would spend a lot of time in. I wasn't planning to try to do much writing. In fact, I have always been the sort of writer who works best out of a predictable routine, and with plenty of order and harmony around him. Brooker showed me his study last. It was a small book-lined room with a desk and two straight-backed chairs, and with exactly the harried, busy-paper look you'd expect it to have. "I've been working on something," he said to me, and took one of the pages from his desk. On the wall above the desk were photographs of Brooker among the powerful; and of his wife, wearing something flowing and diaphanous and white, in various balletic attitudes obviously meant to appear candid, and just as obviously posed for. Brooker apparently caught my interest in these photographs, for he put the page back down and touched the corner of the nearest photograph—of Helen standing in a bath of white light, her slender arms almost hidden in the liquid folds of the gown. He moved the frame just so, and then stared at the picture.

"Helen wanted to be an actress for a while," he said. "She wasn't bad."

"She's beautiful," I said, and realized that I was sounding more and more like a love-struck high school boy.

Rather dryly, Brooker said, "Yes, we agreed about that before." And then, giving me a fatherly smile: "I can bear any number of repetitions concerning the beauty of my wife, lad."

We went downstairs, and I declined what was—I was certain

—a decidedly halfhearted offer of another drink; in any case, I thought it was time to leave. He stood in the light of the landing and asked if I was okay to drive, and I assured him I was, though I had my doubts. As much as I love the taste of bourbon, I have never been able to drink more than a glass or two without getting very unsteady on my feet. When I pulled out onto the highway there was an immediate blurring of the lines of the road ahead, and I held tight to the wheel, going very slow, feeling more sloshed every second.

Mrs. Sweeney was sitting under her yellow porch light, with her flyswatter and her book. She stood and walked over to me.

"My goodness," she said when I staggered.

I took her husband's tie off and held it out to her.

"I don't want it," she said.

I put it into the suit-coat pocket. "I'm sorry," I said. "I've had a little too much to drink."

"Your wife called," she said. "I waited up to tell you."

"You're very kind," I said.

"They showed pictures," Mrs. Sweeney said. "On the news. They showed him being taken into court. He was covering his face."

There wasn't anything I could think of to say to this.

"It was on the news. They think he killed a lot of little kids and buried them somewhere. I was married to him all that time."

I shook my head, and looked out at the road.

"Your wife called," she said. "I told her I'd wait up."

"Thank you, Mrs. Sweeney—and I wish there was something I could say about all this—"

"It's on the news," she said. "It's a big news story."

"I'll watch for it."

"They're going to come talk to me. The news people. They're going to ask me if I knew anything." She shook her head, turning. "You think you know a person."

In the room, I thought of calling Elaine, but what I did was lie across the bed, still wearing the borrowed suit, and, dreaming of a woman twenty years older than I was, I fell deeply, drunkenly asleep.

In the morning I woke to see a shadow move across my window, high up. I lay there with a dry mouth and a headache, watching it for a while, and finally I decided to investigate. As I came to my feet, I thought I heard Mrs. Sweeney's voice, and then other voices. Outside, across the way, on the grassy hill that led onto the interstate ramp and above which the sun had just risen, men were walking. Their shapes were all blazingly outlined, but I could see that they were combing the ground, searching. Mrs. Sweeney stood in the gravel lot, talking to one man while another filmed her, and there were police cars and news-media vans blocking the entrance to the motel. I went back into my room and turned on the television set, but it was too late for morning news; it was all movies and situation comedies and quiz shows. I started to go back out, and then decided not to. I didn't want to see whatever they would find out there, if they found anything at all.

IV

THERE was all that work to do on the house, and I was gone a lot during the next couple of days. I had an excuse to be gone, and I took it. One late night I arrived to find Mrs. Sweeney waiting up for me. She wanted to tell me about the interview with the news people, and her voice as she spoke was an exact blend of excitement and horror. The men searching the hillside had found nothing, she said. To think that murdered children might have been buried within yards of her own house; to think that she had been on the nightly news. "I told them," she said. "I made them understand that when Eddie lived with me he never did anything like hurting a little child."

"It's an awful thing," I said.

"I wrote a letter to my son. I don't know how to tell him."

"Would you like me to look at it?" I said.

She seemed puzzled by such a suggestion. "No," she said.

"Well, anything I can do to help."

She thanked me, but something about my offer to read the letter had made her nervous. I think she considered its contents too private even for the eyes of the faraway young man to whom it was addressed. The next day I stayed around the motel—I took a swim in the pool, and basked in the late-morning sun—and Mrs. Sweeney was uncharacteristically cool and distant. When she came to ask if I wanted lunch, I thought she was almost wary of me. I said I wasn't hungry, and thanked her, then went back to my room, certain that removing myself for the moment was the best thing for her peace of mind. In the room I napped and read magazines, and watched television. Mrs. Sweeney's husband was big news, all right. The authorities were turning up bodies all over the country. When I called Elaine, I told her about the man whose tie I now apparently owned, and though she feigned interest, I could tell that she was restive, wanted to hang up.

"So," I said, "Tell me about your day."

"I studied."

"Anything else?"

"Nothing else."

"No movies? No television? No talk with friends?"

"I said nothing else."

"Is there anything you'd like to talk about?"

"You were telling me about the mad killer-rapist."

"Did I tell you about Brooker's wife?"

"Tell me about Brooker's wife."

"I'm in love with her."

"Wonderful."

"We're going to run away to Paris."

"Terrific."

"We're madly, desperately, spiritually and physically in love."

"I'm very happy for you."

"Elaine," I said.

"You have my blessing," she said.

"Are you coming out in August?" I asked. "We'll have their place all to ourselves."

"We can play Pretend."

"We can do anything you want," I said.

"All I know how to do is study."

"Are you coming out or not?" I said.

"Not."

"Come on, Elaine."

"Not, I'm afraid, is the truth."

"All right," I said, "why not?"

"Maybe I've decided I don't want to live in Virginia."

I didn't say anything then.

"What if I don't like Virginia?" she said.

"Elaine, you loved it. Remember? You picked out the house. You were all excited about fixing it up. I've been working on it all this time."

"I guess I'm getting cold feet. It's senior syndrome, or something."

"Are you serious?" I said.

"Half."

"You mean it."

"A little, yes."

"Are you telling me you might not come out here at all?"

"I don't know what I'm telling you. Don't badger me."

"I have a place for us both to stay until the house is ready. It's a very nice place, Elaine. It's luxurious, in fact."

"And it's famous."

"I don't understand your attitude about this. Yes, it is William Brooker's apartment, and William Brooker is widely known."

"He's famous."

"All right, goddammit, he's famous. Yes."

"Don't get mad," she said. "I'm too tired for anger over the telephone."

"Elaine," I said, "what's the matter?"

She paused, then sighed. "Nothing."

"No," I said, "what's the matter. Tell me."

"Nothing's the matter. I'm tired, and I don't feel like making any big decisions now, all right? I don't want to think about moving and all that. I'm trying to finish up a degree."

"All right, fine," I said.

She said, "Terrific."

We hung up simultaneously, I think. Then I called her back. We traded apologies and explanations. We were both under a lot of pressure; it was a new job, a new situation. She was so tired and beaten down by the work. She had been having anxiety attacks, and was beginning to wonder what it had all been for. I had upset her by talking about child murders and rape, and now the idea of living in a place where such things happened made her tremble. "I know, things like that happen anywhere, but I still feel jittery about living there and I was feeling jittery about it before you told me this horror story."

"It's just nerves," I said. "It's just getting settled, that's all. Once you get settled you'll see."

But in the silence that followed, I wondered if there weren't something more than nerves bothering her.

"Elaine?" I said.

"I don't know," she said. "I don't want to talk now. We'll talk later."

And again, we hung up almost simultaneously.

IN the morning, I had breakfast in Mrs. Sweeney's small diner-kitchen. There were five or six other people staying at the motel now, and she was too busy to speak to me, except to say that her cook, Clara, would be coming back on in a few days, and it couldn't be a minute too soon. She made a gesture like a swoon of exhaustion. Outside, cars slowed going by, or pulled in and sat idling while the curious got out to stare and take pictures. Mrs. Sweeney's husband was a national story now—and each day brought new revelations about him: he had been killing people, mostly little girls, all his adult life. He had drifted across the country, killing as he went, years before settling in Virginia with Marilee Wilson. The psychiatrists who were conducting interviews with him found that he was completely without remorse, without any sense of the enormity of his crimes, and when he spoke about his victims he was chillingly direct and simple, a man describing uncomplicated work, something about which there were only the barest considerations of technique. Police officers from seven states would be converging on the small town jail where he was presently incarcerated; they would all be about the business of talking to the killer to clear away open files, unsolved cases. Some were guessing that it might take years for all the crimes to come to light, and estimated that the numbers were well into the hundreds.

Mrs. Sweeney was glad that business was better, but weary of all the questions, and she didn't like being stared at. The day her husband's picture appeared on the cover of a newsmagazine, she closed her shutters and put up the NO VACANCY sign.

"I don't care about the business anymore," she told me. "I think I'll sell the place now, anyway."

This was about a week before I checked out. I hadn't told her yet that I would be leaving before the September date we had initially agreed on. She had come over from her place on the stoop, and headed me off from a night walk. We stood outside my room and watched the lights on the interstate beyond the crest of the hill across the way. "I used to get lonesome for him," she said, "nights like this."

I had the feeling that she was lonesome for him *now,* but I said nothing.

"Were you on your way somewhere?" she said.

"I was going to take a walk."

"It's a pretty night for a walk."

"Would you like to come with me?" I said, and knew immediately that I had embarrassed her again. "I mean I wouldn't mind company."

She mumbled something about having too much to do.

"Well," I said.

"You know what?" she said. "I don't believe him. I lived with him for three years. If he was like they say he was he would've killed *me*, wouldn't he?"

I said that seemed logical.

"But maybe with someone like that, there isn't really any logic to go by."

"That's probably true," I said.

"I'm going to sell this place and move out of the state." She walked off toward her yellow-lighted stoop.

I watched her go into the office, saw her shadow in the window, and there was something so bowed and unhappy and reproachful about the way she stood gazing out at me that I decided against the walk. I didn't want to find her waiting for me when I returned. I was sorry for everything, but I was in fact a little tired of her trouble; I had troubles of my own. I got into my car and drove over to the rental house, and worked for a few hours painting the rooms. While I worked, I thought about Elaine, and then I was thinking about Brooker's wife. It started as an idle daydream, but I found myself putting embellishments on it, and soon enough I was engaged in a full-fledged fantasy. I imagined that she drove by in the night and saw me in the curtainless windows of the rental house, that she came to the door and knocked, and I let her in. We strolled through the house, talking about what I planned to do with it once Elaine and I moved in, and then we said things that led to kissing. I was on a stepladder, with a roller in my hand, dripping paint, and I realized that I had been quite motionless, deep in this fantasy, for some time. I had seen myself removing Helen Brooker's white cocktail dress, sliding the straps down her shoulders, and I had kissed the soft untanned places on her belly. "Are you a womanizer?" she had asked me that night in her kitchen.

Before I was through, I imagined visiting her at the apartment—saw her arriving early from her travels while I was still alone and sleeping in her bed; I played out a small lubricious drama in which I told her that Elaine was staying behind, would not be joining me, and in which Helen Brooker became my mistress, visiting me every day in the rental house, full of appetite for me and the excitement of our illicitness. In other words, I conjured up a woman who bore no real relation to Helen Brooker—a dream woman who wished only to satisfy my whims.

When, a week later, I carried my suitcases up the sidewalk and the stairs to the landing of Brooker's apartment, I kept my eyes averted for fear of catching a glimpse of his wife, as if to see her would be to cause the whole business to come blurting out of me, the confession of a secret and obsessive lust; for I had kept my fantasies about her, had added to them, had suffered them in my sleep, along with crazy shifts of logic in which the mad mass killer Mr. Sweeney appeared, always in the guise of someone quite harmless at first, and then simply as himself, crouched in a kind of striped, shadowy corner, staring out. I had awakened from these dreams with a jolt, and with the sense that I had come into an area of my life that was utterly uncharted and dark. I found myself deciding against calling Elaine, or putting it off, and when she called me I was as uncommunicative and anxiety-ridden as she was. We had a few very unhappy, very gloomy discussions of plans for the end of summer, and we still hadn't established what she would do. For the time being, I was to move into the Brookers' apartment alone.

When I said goodbye to Mrs. Sweeney, she seemed oddly relieved to have me go. Her son was coming home on leave, she said, and it was too bad I wouldn't be able to meet him.

"Maybe I'll come visit," I said.

"That would be very nice," she said. But I think she was only being polite. I was the last of her customers, and she was closing up for good. She had even let Clara go. She told me this almost as an afterthought: it was too bad that someone like Clara had to go off and work for one of the big places, like Holiday Inn. She didn't think a big chain would appreciate someone of Clara's gifts. Everything was so cut-and-dried these days. She went on like this, tallying up my bill, and I knew she was glad I was leaving.

I didn't have to worry about seeing Brooker's wife, for she was already on her way north. Brooker told me this as he helped me inside with my things. He gave me his key, then called a taxi to come take him to the airport. When I offered to drive him there, he said, "Well, I should've thought of that. The taxi's on its way, though."

"Call and cancel it," I said. "I don't mind taking you."

He considered for a moment. "If you're sure about this, lad."

In the car, I caught the odor of alcohol on his breath. He sat staring out the passenger window, and I coasted along trying to think of something to say to him. I had hoped we might talk on the way, that I might get to know him better. Finally I said, "Will you be meeting your wife in New York?"

"I'm going to Toronto first. Overnight."

"Will she be at Chautauqua with you?"

"Part of the time, maybe. She has friends in the city— Chautauqua's a little too Victorian for her taste."

"Will you be lecturing about the Kennedy years?"

"Some."

"I wish I could've been around for some of that time."

"It wasn't all it was cracked up to be."

"You knew John Kennedy pretty well, didn't you?"

"He was my boss for a while. I knew him, all right."

"He looks so brilliant in all the films—you know, the speeches."

Brooker said nothing to this.

"Everybody who knew him wrote a book about him," I said. "Why didn't you?"

"I decided instead to give lectures. It means more money over a longer period of time. The colleges will pay handsomely for somebody like me to come tell them what they already suspect. After you get famous, lad, you'll be paid handsomely to come read from your work—it's a lot like that. All fiction. Don't tell anyone I said so, but the colleges are full of stupid, limited people, with a very few exceptions. And to be blunt about things, I might as well tell you that it's entirely possible I won't be teaching at our quaint little peaceful school after next year."

"Why not?" I said, breathing the alcohol again. And even so, I thought he would tell me about some grant or other, or plans to spend a year abroad. What he did say was so surprising that I took my eyes off the road a moment to look at him.

"It seems that I'm to be removed—for a few small indiscretions."

I was speechless.

"You must've noticed that I'm inclined to be a bit careless what I say."

If I could've said anything at all, I would have. I sat there staring out at the road and waiting for him to go on.

"The wife and I used to booze it up pretty good. She's got a lot better than I am, of course. But the two of us made a few powerful enemies. It doesn't matter now, you know, because I'm getting near retirement anyway. I guess you're wondering why I'm telling you all this."

"No," I said stupidly, as if I might've expected him to confide in me.

"The truth of the matter is that I did want to salvage something if I could. I mean I hoped that by showing some college spirit I might be able to persuade the Board to reconsider, but I don't think that's going to happen."

"They're *firing* you?" I said.

"Not exactly."

"You're tenured," I said, "aren't you?"

"I never accepted tenure, lad. I didn't want it. I've had a series of special contracts, each year."

I had pulled into the airport terminal. There was a small knot of people at the far gate, and I drove toward it. He already had the door open. "I hope you'll forgive me for deceiving you about—well, about the work. I do like your stories, but I only read them to make this last try, so to speak. I mean I know you thought I was just one of those prescient types who read everything. I searched them out and read them because Helen thought it might impress the Board. I'm afraid it didn't even impress *you* quite as much as I could've hoped it would."

I had stopped the car.

"I guess not," he said, giving me a look.

I got out and helped him with his things, and when he was in line, waiting to board the plane, he shook my hand and told me to make myself at home in his place. I was to use everything just as if it were mine, and he would telephone now and again, if it was all right, just to be sure there wasn't any important mail, or phone calls that needed immediate attention. When I left him there, and started the drive back to town and my new surroundings, I felt as though I had been duped. And I don't mean I was bothered by the fact that he hadn't come upon my work in the course of his normal habits of reading—that had been too outlandish to believe in the first place, and I had indeed been a little embarrassed all along at my own wish to take him at his word; this is hard to explain, muddied as it is by hindsight. In any case, my sense of having been duped had, oddly, to do with Brooker's attitude in the few moments just before I left him at the airport. It was as if I were somehow a creation of his; as if everything I had thought and felt in the few days since I first met him at the faculty orientation party had been produced, orchestrated by him, with calculation and in the certain knowledge that each gesture, each wave of his baton would bring another shade of admiration out of me. I must have looked like an adoring boy at that first meeting.

In any case, I returned to the empty apartment with a very strong sense of dissatisfaction and displeasure concerning Mr. William Brooker. I had decided that if he was a man who deserved my respect, he was not the man of great qualities that I had imagined him to be. And when, that evening, I took his wife's picture down from the wall and carried it with me into her reading room with its small, flower-fragrant bed, I thought of him with something like the mixture of pity and disdain that an adulterer feels for the man he has cuckolded.

V

ELAINE decided not to come until the first of September—the original moving date. I took this news quietly. I had stopped all work on the rental house. I had stopped going out; I was spending each day in the rooms of that apartment, watching television, reading, sleeping, and gazing at what I could find of photographs and belongings of Helen Brooker. I found a box of pictures of her as a girl, and as a bright young student; I found honors and trophies she had won in college, for her work in the yearly stage play, or for her contributions to the literary magazine; I found a stack of lurid-looking paperback books on a shelf in her closet; and, best of all, I found a bundle of old letters and cards in the back of a bureau drawer—birthday greetings, Christmas cards, cards to accompany flowers, and a few thank-you notes, along with letters from her mother, from a sister in Connecticut, and, to my great fascination, from an ardent somebody who kept complaining that she never paid him enough attention. These love notes or complaints were all signed with the initial *W*.

Darling, one of them went, *I suppose you'll laugh when I say this, but someday you'll read what I've written to you, and remember me as your one truest friend; and you'll miss me. On that day you won't laugh. And wherever I am, I'll still love you. Always, W.*

Another said, *Helen, I have written a poem called "Sorry." It's about us. You said to keep in touch, and this is the only way I know how. The poem is simple: Could you spend Sunday / or just any one day / with me / she said / "Sorry." It goes on in this vein, so you see, Helen, I am not without humor concerning you and me. Love, W.*

It suddenly dawned on me as I read that *W* probably stood for William, and that these sophomoric and romantic missives were from the then senatorial staff worker William Brooker, already in his forties and sounding like a nineteen-year-old boy with a crush on his English teacher.

Helen, there's something in your eyes that makes me unable to speak, and the only thing I have is pen and paper. I'm not a poet, but if I were I'd find the words to make you see what happens to me every time you turn your head my way. I love you, Always, W.

This snooping of mine was exactly as undignified and sneaky as it sounds, and I suppose the only thing to be said about it now, once having admitted this, is that it was also a function of a kind of madness that had taken hold of me. At night I had begun to dream about Helen Brooker in a way that left me exhausted in the mornings, and there was always the haunting and shadowy figure of Sweeney, always the terrible fact of his passionless violence in the dreams. I had taken to following the development of the case on the local television stations, two of which were doing specials about him; and there were the continuing newspaper articles. And so in fact, Mr. Sweeney was part of the daytime, too. In the newspaper articles the reporters said Sweeney spoke in a soft, countrified voice about stabbing a girl through the heart, and my own heart shook in my chest, and yet I couldn't look away or stop reading or put my mind on my work. And when I wasn't following the news, I stalked the house for a woman's privacy.

When Elaine and I talked on the phone, our silences grew

longer, and the suppressed irritations began to find terms of expression. We argued, or bickered, or teased each other into bickering, and finally she suggested that something was wrong with us which a separation might solve: she wanted to wait through the fall before coming east, if she came east at all. We could see how we felt in six months. I don't know if she thought much would change in that time, but I felt as though we were dissolving the marriage over the telephone, and I told her so. Her response was a very calm denial that this was so; she just wanted a little time. I even offered, near the end of the conversation, to come west; I said I was willing to give up the job. But of course this was a ridiculous idea, and in any case I didn't think I could bring myself to go through with it. If she wanted me to—which she did not.

So after a week in Brooker's apartment, I was fairly crazed: I was sure my wife was divorcing me; I was having a fantasy affair with a woman I had met only once in my life (there was something about being among her things; it was as if I were a ghost, haunting another ghost, and there was always the feeling that I *did* know her after all), and I was monitoring with avid and horrified fascination the story of Mr. Sweeney and his many victims. To put it simply, I was in no condition for what took place at the end of that first week. And to spare you any unnecessary suspense, I'll just say here that what happened was that I had a visitor, a woman I'd never seen before, someone close to my age or younger, who stood in the light of the Brookers' landing and stared at me as if I had materialized out of the summer night.

I had been reading Brooker's vaguely plagiaristic love notes *(Helen, nothing is as intensely delicate as you are)*, when the doorbell rang, so loudly and so suddenly—it seemed the tolling that calls the guilty to their punishment—that I let out a cry and nearly fell from the chair in which I sat, the letters and notes in a loose bundle on my lap. I almost dropped them all as I came to my feet, and for a confused minute I didn't know what to do with them; I thought this visitor would surely be Helen, or Brooker himself, and that I would be caught red-handed with the evidence of my spying. Finally I jammed everything under a cushion of the sofa and went to the door to peer out at whoever it was. In the dim light of the landing I made out enough of the face to know it wasn't either of the Brookers.

I opened the door.

She stared at me for some time before she spoke. "I am looking for Mrs. Brooker." As I have said, she was my age or younger, and she looked Spanish—her hair was very black, her eyes a facetless black. "I know they live here."

"Mrs. Brooker isn't here," I said.

She looked down a moment, apparently deciding something. Then she simply turned and started back down the steps.

"Excuse me," I said.

She stopped, looked back at me. "You are her son?"

I shook my head no.

"I need to talk to *her*, not him. You tell him that Maria Alvarez came to see Mrs. Brooker. You tell him that."

"Mr. Brooker is in New York State," I said.

"Remember the name," she said, going on, "Maria Alvarez."

I stood out on the landing and watched her cross the parking lot, moving very slowly, almost warily, as if she were afraid someone might spring out at her from behind one of the parked cars. But then it wasn't quite like that, either—for there was an element of discouragement about it, a kind of defeated dignity that made me wonder where she had come from and what she might be going back to. I almost called to her, though of course she probably would not have come back. She got into a small, beat-up Volkswagen bug and drove away, and I went back into Brooker's apartment and took up my invasion of Helen Brooker's personal life.

That evening, Brooker called, and I told him about his wife's visitor.

"Jesus Christ," Brooker said. "Jesus Christ."

I waited.

"Slight Spanish accent?"

"Yes," I said.

"And she asked for *Mrs.* Brooker?"

"Yes."

"Jesus Christ."

"She drove away in an old Volkswagen bug."

"Well, for Christ's sake."

I said nothing. For a moment there was just the faint interference on the line of another, distant conversation.

"Listen," he said. "If she comes back, tell her Mrs. Brooker and I are separated. Okay? We're not living together anymore."

I stood there holding the receiver to my ear.

"Got that?" he said.

"You're separating?" I said.

He took a moment. "Just tell her that. Will you tell her that for me?"

I heard myself say I would.

"Did you tell her when we'd be home?"

"That didn't come up."

"Good."

"She probably won't be back," I said.

"Well, if she *comes* back, you'll remember to tell her Mrs. Brooker and I are separated. We've been separated for some time, you don't know how long."

"Mr. Brooker," I said, "are you asking me to lie for you?"

He took another moment to answer. "Just tell her we're separated. That'll be the truth."

"All right," I said.

"And then call me at this number if she does come back."

"I will," I said to him.

And then he had hung up. I sat for a long time by the phone, not really thinking about anything, and yet feeling low and lonely and sick at heart. Finally I called Elaine.

"Honey," I said, "I miss you."

She had fallen asleep studying, and was groggy and irritable. "Call me back," she mumbled, "okay?"

"Elaine, I'm going crazy here," I said.

"Call me back," she said sleepily, and then the line clicked.

THE afternoon newspaper, in the third part of a four-part series about Mr. Sweeney, carried a summary of his early life. Apparently Mr. Sweeney had been raised by a self-styled freethinker, a man who believed in exposing children early to the realities of life, particularly the sexual realities: the senior Mr. Sweeney had made his young son take part in his own sexual escapades, had made him watch while he and the boy's mother and a friend of the boy's mother had relations. There were other unpleasant details: in Sweeney's own words, he could never be near a living, breathing Human Being without thinking of murder. Mostly, of course, he had chosen little girls because, he said, they were less trouble; everything was easier. In his early twenties he had been married to a young woman for about a month before he killed her, and in his late forties, after almost thirty years of drifting—during which he had spent stretches in prison for petty crimes and felonies, for vagrancy and public drunkenness, and during which he had also lived for a few intermittent years in Canada and Mexico—he had met and married one Marilee Wilson, a motel keeper, who for three years had somehow kept him happy, though he had continued to wander out in search of victims from time to time. In the words of Mr. Sweeney:

I should've probably killed her when we got separated, and I guess I would have if it wasn't for her changing the motel to my name and her boy being such a pal to me. We done a lot of going around, that kid and me, and I come close to telling him more than

*once that his stepdaddy weren't no ordinary stepdaddy. She's a
lucky one, though. She don't know how lucky. I come close more'n
a couple times.*

Reading this, I thought of poor Mrs. Sweeney, who would
certainly have read the same article, and must now be trembling
to think what she had barely missed. And then I was thinking
about them as a couple: there must have been moments of
tenderness between them, moments when they were happy with
each other. Mrs. Sweeney had talked about how she missed
him.

*I almost never can get really excited about sex with somebody
unless they're dead.*

I closed the newspaper and went upstairs to Mrs. Brooker's
room. There were pictures of her on the bed, and I moved them
to the nightstand and lay down. It was warm and bright in the
room, the sun pouring through the chinks in the white curtain
over the window, and through the curtain itself. I had most of
the day ahead of me and I didn't have the energy to move. I
thought of trying to write, but I felt empty, and anyway it would
take energy to write. I could easily have imagined that I might
never have another thing to say. At that moment, nothing
seemed further from me than my own dearest and oldest interest. Indeed, the idea of writing stories seemed somehow so
much beside the point that thinking about it even in this ab-
stract way made me feel foolish.

I tried calling Elaine again, but there wasn't any answer.

Finally I went out, and drove myself over to the Sweeney
Motel. I don't think I intended at first to go there. I remember
I thought about riding around the campus, perhaps stopping in
on one of my new colleagues. But the truth of the matter was
that I hadn't liked any of them much. They had struck me as
a closed group; their conversation in my presence had been full
of in-jokes and references to things I couldn't know and therefore could not respond to. (During my years traveling and
reading at the colleges I have come to see that this is a rudeness

particular to academics, and that my first colleagues were no worse than most.)

So I wound up back at the Sweeney Motel, which was closed now, the windows all curtained and shut and the NO VACANCY sign replaced by a single large wooden plank with the word CLOSED painted on it in black. I pulled in and sat for a minute, looking the place over. Mrs. Sweeney came to her doorway as I got out of the car.

"What is it?" she said.

"Mrs. Sweeney," I said, "how are you?"

"I'm closed," she said. But then she recognized me.

"I just thought I'd—stop by."

She opened the door and stood back for me to enter. I was afraid I'd come at a bad time, and I apologized, or tried to, but she was already talking.

"My son got his leave canceled. And I know why—I wouldn't come here either if it was me."

The office was a mess. There were newspapers and magazines everywhere; on the television cabinet, glasses and dishes were stacked, and the tables were strewn with clothes. There wasn't anywhere to sit. Mrs. Sweeney cleared a place on the sofa, and then poured herself a tall glass of whiskey from one of several bottles of liquor on the coffee table.

"You want some?" she said.

I declined, and she sat down across from me, keeping her eyes on the TV screen, where a doctor and a nurse argued in an antiseptic-looking hallway. She drank her whiskey, licked her lips. It struck me that I had come there to stare at her, that no matter what I'd convinced myself with when I started out, my motives were no better than those of the merely curious. She was watching me, and I couldn't really return the look, couldn't meet her gaze. "So you're all closed up," I managed.

"Nothing else to do. My son's not coming home. I got people calling me all hours of the day and night. Godalmighty, you know *I* didn't kill anybody. It wasn't *me*, goddammit. I don't know anything. All I know is I was married to the guy three years and I never saw him hurt anyone or anything, and if he wasn't a real exciting man to have around the house he wasn't half bad, either. He left me alone mostly and he never expected much. It wasn't such a bad marriage and now I got to feel like I'm going to grow boils and horns if I miss him a little bit every now and then. People coming here wanting to know did he ever do anything that made me suspicious. I've had three husbands in my life and they all had things about them that you couldn't say was too normal. Who doesn't? Who's normal in private? He didn't seem a bit more strange than anybody else is when nobody's looking." She took a long pull of her drink. "Sure you don't want any?"

"No, thank you," I said.

"I'm going to sell this place and move. Change my name back."

"I'm sorry your son isn't coming."

"He doesn't want to be *seen* in this town again."

I shook my head as if to say how unfortunate this was, but she thought I was disagreeing with her.

"I'm serious," she said. "He doesn't want to be seen. He won't ever come back here. He told me he wouldn't, and I can't say I blame him."

"No," I said, "I can understand that."

She stared at the television. There was a commercial on about sheer panty hose, and then there was one about an airline. She took another drink of the whiskey and then leaned back in her chair. "I don't usually drink," she said. "I don't like the taste of it. I've just been taking it to calm down. You know, I just escaped death. More than once. He was going to kill me."

"I—I saw that," I said.

"Everybody saw it. You know he was with a lot of people here. He knew a lot of people and went to restaurants and fishing and all that, and even sat in church every week—we were regulars, the two of us. And nobody else figured out what he was either, if you know what I mean. You'd think *somebody* would've noticed something."

"It's very strange," I said.

"And I'm not going to pretend I didn't like having him around because I did, and I don't care what they say."

I nodded agreement.

"You know," she said, "you're the last tenant of the Sweeney Motel."

"Why don't you just call it The Wilson Motel again?"

She looked a little puzzled. "Oh, it was never The Wilson Motel. It was The All Nighter Motel."

This harmless piece of information had the effect of putting us both in a kind of musing calm. We might indeed have been mother and son, considering some fact or circumstance that had caught our attention. I reached over and poured a little of the whiskey into a cup on the coffee table.

"Let me get you a clean glass," she said.

I sat back and waited for her. On television a man in a bright T-shirt was biting into a hamburger, and the juices went flying. Mrs. Sweeney came back from her small kitchen and handed me a plastic tumbler, then poured far more whiskey than I wanted into it. We drank. I had an abrupt sense of how truly solitary my existence had become in the weeks since my arrival in Virginia.

"Well," Mrs. Sweeney said, "I sure didn't think you'd actually come back and visit me."

I smiled at her and held up my glass, as if to offer a toast.

"You know, I unplugged my phone. I don't even look at the mail, except to see if there's something from my boy."

Mrs. Sweeney had been leading her own solitary existence.

"I've got plenty of room," I said, "where I'm staying."

She swallowed her whiskey and looked at the television screen. "One time Sweeney killed a cat," she said.

I waited.

"We were on our way to Florida and the cat was in the road

and he just pulled right over it—swerved to get it." She took
another swallow. "Just—wham. Like that. No cat. A smear in
the road behind us. And when I asked him why in the world
he'd do a thing like that he said it was because he felt like it."

"So—" I said. "So that was—"

"That was scary," she said. "It scared the hell out of me."

"When was it?"

"Year after we were married."

I drank my own whiskey.

"You know why I divorced him?"

I shook my head.

"The laziness. I couldn't get him to do anything. All he
wanted to do was watch television—Westerns. He loved Westerns. John Wayne and Randolph Scott. Horses and dust, and
leather saddles and boots, and the cowboy hats. And—and
clothes, you know, he loved clothes. He bought stuff he'd never
wear even if he could've got around to it. Shoes and shirts and
ties and belts, and pairs of socks. I couldn't get him to do
anything around here that needed doing, so finally I just told
him to pack his things and get out. Which he did." She was
emphatic now. "Which he did. And he went as peaceful as a
lamb. Now, you tell me."

I was beginning to feel the whiskey. I put my glass down and
stood up. "Mrs. Sweeney, I have plenty of room where I'm
staying—you're welcome to come stay there if you want to get
away from here." I thought this was the least I could do.

"Isn't that nice of you," she said.

I said, "I mean it."

"Well," she said, rising. The whiskey had had its effect on her
as well. She tottered, sat back down. "Stay and watch television
for a while."

I didn't really have anywhere else to go, and yet I made my
excuses and went out to my car, which was blazing hot in the
afternoon sun, and drove back across the campus to William
Brooker's apartment, where I intended to lie down and sleep off

the effects of what I'd had to drink. As I climbed the stairs to the landing, already sweating profusely in the heat, I thought I caught a glimpse of someone peering at me from the other side of the building. When I looked, there wasn't anything, but I was pretty sure I hadn't imagined it. When I was at Brooker's door, I looked out at the parking lot, and saw the Volkswagen bug—the same one, with the same battered fender, the same rusty, gouged finish. Inside, in the cool of the air conditioning, I went straight to the bathroom and took a lukewarm shower, my mind made up to ignore all news and all thoughts of the Brookers or Elaine or poor Mrs. Sweeney, and when I was finished I got into Helen Brooker's bed and took a fitful, erotic-dreaming nap: someone, a woman, a spirit, was leading me into a velvet room.

I woke to the sound of the doorbell. It was dark. There was music coming from somewhere; the doorbell kept sounding, and I hurried down the stairs, trying to get my pants up without missing a step, or tripping over my own feet. "Just a minute," I said. I had no shirt; my eyes were sleep-filled and probably swollen. I opened the door, and of course even half asleep I knew it would be Maria Alvarez.

"Mrs. Brooker, please," she said, in that Spanish-soft voice.

"I should've told you—she's out of town," I answered, peering around the door at her. "They've been gone a few days now." And I was not too groggy to add, "They're separated."

She looked at me, then muttered something I couldn't catch.

"Excuse me?" I said.

"Separated?"

I nodded.

"*Sep*arated," she said, looking out at the dark. For perhaps a minute she simply stood there. "Separated." This time it was as if she were trying to hold back a laugh.

"That's right," I said.

"You know this," she said.

"Yes."

"Separated."

"Do you want to come in?" I asked, holding the door open a little more.

"In there?"

"Yes."

She seemed about to laugh again. "You're very kind, but no."

"I'm sorry," I said.

Her eyes took in the room behind me, and her expression seemed now only curious. "Mrs. Brooker—what is she like?"

"Why don't you come in?" I said.

"Mrs. Brooker is nice?"

"Yes."

"A nice woman. Poor Mrs. Brooker." And now she was laughing, though she tried to stifle it, holding her hand over her mouth. "Separated."

"Look," I said, "what is this about?"

She turned and went back down the stairs, still laughing, and when I followed her partway down she only went faster, until she was on the lawn, almost running.

"Miss?" I said. "Miss?" But she went on. The little, ragged-edged old car roared as she pulled out of the lot and on down the street.

THAT night, all night, I spent in Brooker's study, looking through his papers, his photographs, his files, for some sign of this young woman who had wanted to talk to his wife. I thought I knew why she wanted to talk to Helen Brooker, and I believed I understood exactly why Brooker had asked me to do what I had in fact done—to tell the lie that he had doubtless known would send the young woman away. Yet it was a fool thing to think I might find what I was looking for in the study of a man like Brooker, even knowing that he had a weakness for alcohol, and therefore might be expected to be careless; and if I did find the incriminating letter or note, I certainly had no plans for it

—there wasn't anything at all that I could possibly want with it. No, this rummaging through Brooker's papers was only another kind of undignified snooping, and the fact that I found nothing seemed finally to be a sort of judgment of me, as if my nosiness had earned me exactly what I deserved.

Even so, when I finally lay down in Helen Brooker's bed that early morning, I felt elated, and this is perhaps the most difficult thing to explain; I'm not even quite certain that I understand it now. I didn't know Brooker, really, at all: yet I had at his request relayed a bald lie to a young woman who had believed that lie, and then I had spent most of the night searching for evidence that, I suppose, would merely have proved what I felt I already knew—all of this just as undignified as my nocturnal voyeuristic journeys through Helen Brooker's private things . . . and even so, I felt this sense of elation. I remembered Helen Brooker saying to me about Jack Kennedy, "He was an awful womanizer, you know." And perhaps I was merely feeling the excitement of interest, to have been privy to something Brooker would want hidden.

VI

Dearest Helen,

J. says he likes your eyes best. He especially likes tall, leggy types, very smart, very sexy. All of which you are. I think he has designs on you and so you must be very careful this April. I've been working on a speech for the visit to B. Harbor. Lots of ward types down there. I wish you'd call me once in a while; I mean one could get the feeling you're not letting the absence grow your heart fonder, or words to that effect.

Love, W.

Brooker called late the next morning. I had been up for an hour or so, hiding the signs of my recent strangeness—putting Helen Brooker's photographs where they belonged, her letters and cards back in their bundled order (though I had taken the time to copy down a few things to take with me, things I knew would be of interest to me later, most notably the one set out above, with its reference to a J. that simply must be Jack), and rearranging the casual disorder of Brooker's study. I had mostly finished all this—there were just a few envelopes to be put away —and was taking a short break to watch the morning report. (For the first time in many mornings, no mention was made of Sweeney.)

"Well," Brooker said, through the hiss of long distance. "Did she come back?"

"She came back," I said.

"Jesus Christ."

"I told her you were separated."

"Did she buy it?"

I thought of the first time I had seen him, of the confidence with which he had leaned toward me to murmur his obscenity. And then in an odd shift of mind I had an image of that boy behind the counter at the beach house and restaurant, the day I met Elaine.

"Well?" Brooker said.

"She believed what I told her," I said.

"She bought it."

"Yes."

"When did she come back?"

"Last night. I think she's watching this place."

"Jesus Christ."

"Mr. Brooker, what is she to you?"

"Listen, why didn't you call me last night?"

"It was too late. It was late. What is she to you, Mr. Brooker?"

"She's nothing. Don't pay any attention," he said.

"Well, then what does she want?"

After a moment, he said, "She was a student of mine. She had a problem."

I waited.

"She got the wrong idea of things—the way things were. And now she wants to make trouble for me."

"Did you by any chance have an affair with her?"

"She's just a kid," he said.

I could feel the adrenaline running at the back of my neck. "Yes," I said, "but did you?"

After another pause he said, "Look, I appreciate your help. You *do* have the use of my apartment. I don't think that entitles you to make assumptions about my affairs."

"I think I have to know what the situation *is* if I'm going to be of any more help," I said.

There was still another pause. "I told you," he said. "She got the wrong idea of things. There's something unstable about her that I should've seen—she's of *age*, if that's what you're getting at."

"Does your wife know about her?"

"Jesus Christ," he said, "what is this?"

"She says she wants to talk to your wife—she was asking questions about your wife."

"Look, I can't talk about this anymore. You told her we were separated and you said she bought it—did she buy it or not?"

"I guess she bought it," I said.

"Well, then—fine. If she comes back again will you call me?"

"Do you want to talk to her?"

"Jesus Christ, no. Call me *after* she shows up again, if she does. And if she bought what you told her she probably won't."

"All right," I said.

He muttered, "Jesus Christ," then thanked me for my help, and we said goodbye. The line on his end closed; I listened until the dial tone started.

Outside, the parking lot was ablaze, the sun reflecting too brightly off the cars for me to see much. I went out and walked around the building, hoping that I might find her waiting on one of the landings, or behind one of the parched-looking sycamores in the grassy square across from the main entrance. There wasn't a soul, it seemed, anywhere. All the windows of the building were closed against the heat, and the little park for children was empty; a hot breeze disturbed some sheets on a line that had been strung across one of the landings. Cars going by on the road looked as if they were trailing fire.

IN the morning, there was another article about Sweeney. He had talked to police from surrounding states, and apparently all of his stories were checking out; authorities were finding remains where he said he'd left them. In describing these burial sites, the article said, he often fell into a kind of reverie, and his crimes became nouns. *That one, yeah, that would be a knife. And, let's see, oh, this one's a strangle.*

I read all this with the same, sick fascination, and then called Elaine. She was in bed; she had been down with a cold. "I miss you," she said.

I had the TV on, the midday news, and was lying back in Brooker's easy chair with the telephone in my lap. "Elaine," I said, "I'm going out of my mind."

"Maybe our separation isn't going to work out," she said.

"Are you finished with everything?" I asked. And then I didn't hear what she said, because the local news was showing film of Maria Alvarez standing out on the roof of the college library building. I sat there with Elaine's familiar sleepy voice in my ear and understood what I was seeing. It was Maria Alvarez. Before I could get out of the chair, the picture shifted, everything changed: a crowd of police and firemen were gathered around a broken shape under a blanket in the street.

I pulled the telephone from its table, reaching to turn the TV up, and when I did get the sound up there was only the announcer, a man looking far too calm for what his camera crew had just shown, talking about the morning's tragedy with a series of eyewitnesses, who all reported the same thing. The poor girl jumped. They had seen it all; they were afraid, and their voices shook, and the announcer remained calm, holding the microphone to their mouths.

I don't remember what I said to Elaine. It's entirely possible that I blurted out everything I knew of Brooker and his trouble, speaking, no doubt, with that peculiar clarity that horror sometimes provides an otherwise cloudy mind. But it wasn't long before I was dialing the number Brooker had given me, and having trouble accomplishing it because my hands were shaking so. I don't think I quite expected to get through to him at this hour, and I left a little pause of surprise when he answered.

"Yes?" he said.

"What did you do to her, Brooker?"

"Who is this?"

"Did you tell her you were in love with her?"

He said nothing for a moment. Then, "I can't talk now."

"For God's sake," I said, "I *lied* to her for you. My God, I don't believe this—I told her your lie, and sent her on her way. I helped you do it."

"Now, hold on," he said. "She had a lot of trouble—there were things that had nothing to do with me or any lie. For God's sake, what's happened?"

"Jesus Christ," I said.

"Let's calm down," William Brooker said. "Just tell me what she did."

THAT night I slept on the sofa in the guest room. In his horror, Brooker had been fatherly and philosophical: there was nothing to be done, nothing *he* could do, at any rate; he was very sorry for the troubled Miss Alvarez, he had tried his best to help her, but in the end he was powerless. He hadn't known her very well, in fact, and perhaps no one ever really gets to know a suicide. Miss Alvarez had wandered into a seminar he had taught as a visiting lecturer the previous fall in Atlanta, and he had seen right away that she was barely holding on. He described his concern for her, his work with her while she was his student; it was all very much a professional relationship, candid and aboveboard, he said; and of course it was quite clear that he was lying. I told him I couldn't talk anymore, and hung the phone up. I didn't care what he thought about this, and I don't mean that I was as full of moral outrage as I must have sounded. For the facts of the matter are that something had occurred to me concerning my own part in it all, and I simply wanted no more to do with anyone or anything for a time. What occurred to me was the unpleasant truth that I had held something back in the first minute Maria Alvarez had stood staring at me in the dim light of the landing. She had asked to see Mrs. Brooker and I had said only that Mrs. Brooker wasn't there; I had kept back what I knew about where Helen Brooker was and how long she would be gone, and I had done so, without having to think about it, because of course I understood in an instant what Maria Alvarez had come for, and what she would want with William Brooker's wife. I had, then, already begun the lie that Brooker would later ask me to complete—and this not out of friendship for the man, or loyalty to his interests, but out of something else.

In the days that followed, Brooker called two or three times, wanting to get what details he could. I told him I would not be staying in his apartment anymore, and so there were practical things to consider as well. He didn't say much about his own part in the affair, and yet I was able to piece together a version of it from what he *did* say: Maria Alvarez comes to him looking for what she imagines he can give her; she's pathologically unhappy, but he doesn't see this. He sees her shapely figure and Spanish-dark features, her deep black eyes. He charms her, seduces her, then finds that she is quite mad, quite unable to understand the casual way he means this sort of thing, and he decides it is necessary to evade her. The rest is, of course, an unfortunate chain of events over which he has no control. If only the world weren't the way it is. I had no trouble at all imagining the whole scenario.

What I never imagined had to do with Helen Brooker. She showed up on a Friday afternoon from New York, having set out at the request of her husband, to make certain that things were in order for my departure. (We had no signed agreement, and Brooker was a thorough man.) She came breezing into the living room, where I lay on the white sofa in a bath of letters and photographs—the whole history of William and Helen Brooker. She went into the kitchen and poured us both a bourbon, then came and stood over me, holding my drink out, her eyes not quite settling on what I had in my hands and on my lap. I took the drink, and she sipped hers, still standing over me. "I suppose writers have to be spies," she said. "It must be a perfectly seedy little part of the job."

I put my drink on the end table and began to gather up the photographs.

"Did you find anything of interest?" she said.

I said, "No."

"How unfortunate."

"One of the perfectly seedy little risks of the job," I said.

She took another drink. "Do you suppose I ought to look for a way to get you?"

"I guess you'll do what you want to do."

"You're not even sorry, are you."

"Yes," I said, "in fact I am. I'm quite sorry."

"To think I believed you were charming. It turns out you're just a writer."

I had got everything in a stack, and had put it carefully, as if it were fragile, aside. "I wish I could tell you how sorry I *really* am," I said. When I remember this now, it seems clear that I didn't have much respect for her anymore, and it all had to do with what I thought she did not know about her husband.

"Are you referring," she said, "to Miss Alvarez?"

I looked at her. There was nothing at all in her eyes.

"Of course you are."

"You know," I said.

"William has always been like a little child in a candy store when it comes to women." She finished her drink, and then, precisely as though I were no longer there, put away the papers and letters and photographs. I went upstairs and packed my things, and she followed me, stood in the doorway of the room, her room, watching me.

"This is where you slept?"

"Yes."

"That's fascinating."

"I had to sleep somewhere," I said.

"You don't think much of us, do you? Or of me."

I didn't say anything to this.

"I suppose I should go jump off a building, the way that poor girl did."

"Mrs. Brooker," I said, "you wondered if I was sorry about —about prying the way I did. What about you? What about your husband? There's a young woman dead, Mrs. Brooker. What about that?"

"Your indignation is touching," she said.

We didn't say much else to each other before I left. She stood by with the air of someone who has dealt the telling blow, sipping her drink now and again, tapping the toe of one shoe on the hardwood floor. As I went down the stairs she said, "They all deserve whatever they get." It was as if she were hurling it at me as I scurried away; as if she wanted to chase me with it. There was no anger or pain in her voice—only scorn. And my answer was exactly the kind of stupid, reflexive thing one regrets later, thinking of the smart things one could have said if only one had been able to summon the presence of mind, or the courage, or the calm. I said, "I'm sorry I ever saw you." And of course the fact is that if I'd had an hour to think of something I would no doubt have found nothing better: I was to begin a teaching job in less than two weeks, and I couldn't imagine anything I might have to say to anyone.

I drove around the city for a while that evening. I don't know what I thought I might see in those quiet streets, the fine old houses and shaded lawns. I suppose I needed simply to get a feeling for the town as something continuous, something—well, ongoing and unabstract, too: children playing in the splashed blue shade of a sycamore; a dog barking from behind a white picket fence.

When it grew too dark to see, I stopped at a package store and bought myself a bottle of whiskey. I intended to get drunk, of course, but I didn't. I went to the rental house and worked all night painting the bedroom and the guest room. Oh, I had some of the whiskey, all right. I had enough to make me sleep in spite of a feeling so desperate and hopeless that, in the morning when I woke and remembered it, I thought of drinking more of the whiskey to keep it at bay. But it was immediately upon me again, and I made myself go about the business of cleaning up the rooms, even as my conviction grew that I would not be living in that house. I had no sense of it—even with all my work on it—as a place where I might be with Elaine, one of a pair of tenants, at home.

A little later, when I headed over to the Western Union office to wire Elaine for the money to fly back to the Midwest, I had my mind half made up to tell her I was coming back for good, that I would not be taking the job after all. In fact, it was Elaine who, that week, insisted that we go through with everything as planned, that we travel east to take up residence in the rental house.

VII

THAT fall, I saw Brooker now and again, from a distance, as I'm sure most people on the campus ever saw him. He left the

college, that spring, and the faculty bulletin said he was starting
his retirement, along with his lovely wife, Helen, in Key West.
The Sweeney motel was torn down before the year was out, and
I never saw Mrs. Sweeney again. The last thing I heard about
her infamous husband was that he was an object of study: the
doctors were hoping to find some clue to him.

Elaine and I remained in the rental house for almost two
years, and then bought a place, a little bigger, and a lot older,
on the other side of the campus. I would never have believed
that I might stay at a small college like that, but we did stay
more than seven years. All four of our children, two boys and
two girls, were born there. Sometimes at night I wake up from
a dream that I'm holed up in a place like Brooker's apartment,
and then our room feels like a little cave in the dark. If I can't
go back to sleep I get myself up and go look at the children. I
tuck their blankets over their shoulders, remove their books or
toys from their beds; I perform the tasks of a father in the night.
Elaine sleeps so soundly that my kiss never wakes her. Our life
together is full and perhaps often enough a little too busy; there
are times when I think we just miss each other. But that is
probably true of any couple.

Whenever I think of that end of summer so long ago, when
I took flight from an oppression that might have unhinged me,
I remember the slow, lonely hours in the air—the sense that the
world below me was little more than a savage place where the
weak were fed upon by the strong—and the nervous feeling
when I arrived, the fear that my marriage really was over for
all my indulgence in those fantasies of betrayal, and our mutual
neglect. And the way it felt to see Elaine standing in the white
light of the airport terminal, waiting for me.

How good it was to see her.

As I walked up the ramp toward her, lugging my packed
suitcase and my unhappy experience like the same great weight,
I understood at least that I loved her, and I remember my sense
of wonder about this. I remember also that I thought of

Sweeney, and of Brooker; that Sweeney and Brooker occurred to me then as though they were, together, the opposing principle—a naked manifestation of the forces that would always be lurking in the darker corners of the spirit. I put this from my mind, and stepped forward to greet her. "Darling," I said. I couldn't believe how familiar and wonderful she looked.

She smiled as if to say we would be all right now.

There was a thing in us both that moved us in each other's direction, that made us recognizable to each other. Whatever our complications, this obdurate fact remained.

"You look beat," she said, and she reached across the little space that divided us.

Fairfax, Virginia
1984–86

For a complete list of books available from Penguin in the United States, write to Dept. DG, Penguin Books, 299 Murray Hill Parkway, East Rutherford, New Jersey 07073.

For a complete list of books available from Penguin in Canada, write to Penguin Books Canada Limited, 2801 John Street, Markham, Ontario L3R 1B4.